A Rachel Markham Mystery

THE ORACLE OF DEATH

BOOK 7 - IN THE MYSTERY SERIES

A Rachel Markham Mystery

THE ORACLE OF DEATH
BOOK 7 - IN THE MYSTERY SERIES

P.B. KOLLERI

Notion Press

Dedicated to Dr. George King
With love

Then God pitied him,
He made him very rich.

~ The Hymn to Dionysos, The Homeric Hymns

Chapter One

THE GREEK ISLANDS.

AUTUMN, 1948.

The storm raged on the sea, tearing the waves apart and bringing them up to crests, such as they had never ridden, before sending them crashing with unbearable violence onto the shore. Twilight had set in. Stanley Papanos stood and watched from the window of his luxurious beach house, high up on the cliff, as a small wooden boat was bodily lifted out of the Aegean Sea and smashed to smithereens on the rocks below. He thought to himself with a grim satisfaction, 'sometimes even the Gods come down and give one a helping hand.' He wanted solitude and the storm offered him just that. No one could reach the island by boat or by seaplane in such a tempest.

But even that thought, comforting as it was, could not quell the waves of grief that were moving through his body, as though they were a manifestation of a restless physical pain. Stanley Papanos, one of the heirs to the multimillion dollar Papanos shipping empire, had just turned thirty-four. Born to a Greek father and an English mother, his features were decidedly bland by Greek standards, as was his light brown hair and medium light skin tone. Although he would be considered tall, dark and handsome, in a foreign sort of way, in any English drawing room with his six-foot stature, his athletic build, a perfectly shaped Greek nose and brown eyes, by Greek standards he was still no Adonis.

As peals of thunder reverberated through the air and synchronised with the sound of the crashing waves, a thousand branches of lightening flashed across the sky. He continued to gaze out the window. His usually calm features were twisted in agony as he thought to himself, how could one human being inflict so much misery on another. If only he had listened to his family and not married the woman. They had all warned him against doing so. The woman he had loved body and soul with an unworldly passion. The same woman who had nearly destroyed him, the love of his life, his bewitching wife – Ariana.

A door discretely opened behind him and he could smell a familiar perfume. This person turned on the lamps in the room with a flick of a switch, chasing away the twilight and replacing it with a warm golden light. Without turning, he asked, 'What is it, Grandmamma?'

'Nerissa says she called you twice. Dinner is getting cold. And I would like some company.'

He answered gruffly, his gaze still upon the waves, 'I told Nerissa I didn't want any dinner. And I'm afraid, I'm not very good company either at the moment.'

Aristea Papanos spoke in a steely voice, 'Pull yourself together, child! What's been done is done. It's all over now.'

Stanley turned to look at her in astonishment. She was a powerhouse packed in a deceptively delicate, eighty-five-year-old body. She possessed what some would call an immense presence. Standing at 5' 2", her matriarchal personality still towered over him. Her dark eyes flashed and the few wrinkles around her eyes belied her age. Her beautiful oval face was framed by her perfectly coiffed dyed jet black hair, which suited her warm olive complexion.

She wore a flowing Greek kaftan in muted shades of olive and beige silk. She sat down near him, making herself comfortable in an antique armchair covered with faded golden brocade. The light from the lamps, filtered by dull gold shades, reflected back from her dark eyes and endowed them with a strange golden gleam.

He asked slowly, 'Oh, my God! You've killed Ariana, haven't you?'

'Don't be so stupid. Do I look like a murderer?'

'Then how do you know it is all over?'

Aristea spoke, measuring her words carefully, 'As the head of this family, I make it my business to know everything.'

Stanley gave a hollow laugh. 'Then you should know that nothing is over. It is just the beginning. I got a call from the police in Athens an hour ago, from a certain police lieutenant - Ari Demakis of the Hellenic Gendarmerie. He was asking about Ariana's whereabouts. It seems that certain rumours floating about in the village, have reached the mainland.'

Aristea scoffed, 'Police! It will take them at least two days to arrive. This storm has already been raging for the past twenty-four hours and it still shows no sign of letting up. Mark my words, it will last another day, if not two. By then the sea will have destroyed all evidence.'

'Oh my God! What have you done?'

'Don't be a fool, Stanley! We have done nothing. Nothing! You understand? Ariana brought it all upon herself. Some may call it destiny. I call it justice. Now, pull yourself together and help your poor grandmother out of this chair.'

Stanley walked over to her and helped her up. For all the power of her personality, she did feel frail on his arm. She got up with difficulty and latched on to his forearm and he allowed himself to be led out of the room by her.

As they walked slowly down the arched, whitewashed hallway towards the dining room, Aristea spoke, 'Your brother - Stavros, called from London. He said he would return next week. The deal with the Nordic shipping corporation came through. He is very pleased.'

'He would be,' Stanley said tonelessly.

'And he mentioned that he is bringing some friends from England back with him, so we need to prepare for houseguests.'

Stanley groaned. 'Tell him to put them off, please! For my sake.'

'Well, we can't do that. I am sorry. They would have already set sail by now.'

'Who are these friends? Do we know them?'

'I don't think so. Stavros mentioned that they were a couple. And that the man was an old room-mate from his Oxford days. Someone called Jeremy Richards. I forget his wife's name. But they will be staying with us.'

Stanley looked puzzled. 'Richards. Jeremy Richards. The name sounds familiar. Now, where have I heard it before?'

'Not in Greece, of that you can be sure. He did mention that this would be their first ever trip to Greece,' Aristea said, as they entered the high ceilinged, domed dining room.

Stanley spoke, 'Yes. That could be but I am certain I've heard that name before.'

'Perhaps Stavros mentioned it when he came back from Oxford?'

Stanley shook his head. 'No, that was years ago. And I am quite sure this was more recent.'

As she gingerly lowered herself into the dining chair, which Stanley courteously held out for her, Aristea spoke with a smile, 'Ah, well, it will probably come to you once you take your mind off of it, which I would advise you to do now. Our dinner is waiting. And thankfully, it still smells delicious.'

And Stanley found himself thinking, how deftly she had managed to steer the conversation away from Ariana. Women of the species were definitely deadlier than the male. Or perhaps the streak of ruthlessness, which seemed to run in his family, had somehow missed him by inches. He couldn't quite decide whether he was thankful for that or not.

Chapter Two

Athens was a sunny, colourful and delightful alternative for the senses after grey and wintry England. Rachel and Jeremy had arrived in Greece the night before, for a fortnight's holiday on Stavros Papanos' invitation and were out sightseeing on their first day in Athens.

Jeremy's friend, Stavros had provided them with a guide - a young Greek man in his twenties named Yanni, who worked as a junior clerk with Papanos Shipping. He was an eager to please, pleasant young man, who described the sights to them with great enthusiasm, in a smattering of English mixed with Greek that was easy for both Jeremy and Rachel to understand.

Having taken in the sights, sounds and smells of Athens, and having spent hours trudging in and around the magnificent Acropolis, the Parthenon and a walk around the temples of Athena and Poseidon, Rachel and Jeremy were now in the grounds below the Acropolis.

As they walked through the ruins of Agora- the ancient marketplace below the Acropolis, Rachel said enthusiastically, 'Just think, we are walking on the same path that Socrates or Pythagoras themselves must have taken, a thousand times, as they pondered over philosophical truths and mathematical theorems. These are the very people that gave us the very first concepts of mathematics, theatre, medicine, philosophy and democracy. These are the hallowed grounds, this is where it all happened, the birthplace of western civilisation, as we know it!'

Jeremy gave her an amused look and said, 'Yes, and to think that the pebble in my shoe might have been the same stone Socrates kicked as he came up with the philosophy of moderation in everything, including not getting carried away with our imaginations.'

Rachel grinned. 'Point noted. I suppose I've been waxing poetic all morning but it is hard to be here and not get carried away.'

Turning to their guide, Rachel asked, 'What do you think, Yanni?'

Yanni shrugged and gave a shy smile, 'To be honest, I live here. So, I don't think much about it. It's all part of the scenery to us. Merely tourist attractions.

But according to me, there is a place even more special than this and I would like to take you there.'

He had their interest.

He informed them that apart from the main tourist attractions, he wanted to show them places that few tourists knew of. After the visit to the museum, he took them to Plaka, the old part of Athens and from there, he took them up a path that led to a charming little village called Anafiotika. Rachel was delighted.

After the splendour and grandeur of the Acropolis, Parthenon and Agora, walking through the narrow winding lanes of Anafiotika, or little Anafi, was like sipping a glass of mellow wine after a long tiring yet satisfying day. Yanni told them that this quiet little village was mostly occupied by people from the island of Anafi who had come to seek livelihood in Athens, after the Greeks regained their independence from the Ottoman Empire.

The narrow pathways were lined with stark whitewashed homes, a profusion of potted flowers, oleanders and cats lazing in the sunshine. Windows and doors were painted with bright colours from Mediterranean blue to cherry red and Rachel thought this was one of the most charming places she had ever seen. As they walked up the winding hill, she could see people tending their yards, or just enjoying their evening coffee. Most of the residents often stopped what they were doing to give them a friendly wave as they walked by. This was the idyllic laid-back side of the otherwise bustling Athens and Jeremy stopped to take pictures of the view from the hill every now and then.

Then they walked back to Plaka, where they did some souvenir shopping in the touristy shops and taverns, which lined the cobblestoned streets of Plaka. Rachel had bought herself a peasant blouse made of white cotton, embellished with colourful embroidery on the square neck line and a flouncy multi-coloured Greek skirt. Jeremy picked up film for his new camera.

Rachel's boundless energy had finally run out after all the walking they had done and she requested Yanni if they could get a drink and a bite to eat somewhere. Yanni said he knew just the thing that would revive them and took them to an eatery in Monastiraki Square where they found an old wooden bench to sit on and within minutes, Yanni came back holding two enormous conical snacks wrapped in paper and handed them over to Rachel and Jeremy. 'Try this. It is a savoury Greek snack called souvlaki. It is filling and refreshing at the same time.'

Rachel took a big bite of the souvlaki and her eyes widened with the sensory delight of experiencing her first souvlaki. Forgetting her manners, she asked Yanni with her mouth full, 'This is incredible. What is it made from?'

Yanni grinned, 'I thought you will like this. Souvlaki is, how you say, meat grilled on a skewer, wrapped up in pita bread along with salad, spices and tzatziki – a thick sauce made with yogurt, garlic and cucumber. It is very popular with the locals. I've also ordered some local wine for us.'

The sun was setting and a street musician in traditional Greek attire started playing the mandolin, not far from where they sat. As the soulful strains of his music reached their ears, and the souvlaki satisfied their hunger, a golden glow stretched across the skies and Rachel felt she was indeed in a sensory heaven created by the Greek Gods themselves.

The wine was young yet full bodied and they enjoyed sipping it as they watched people go by. By the time they returned to the Papanos guesthouse, an old ornate building situated in the heart of Athens, it was dark outside.

As they entered, they were greeted by the sight of an agitated Stavros, pacing up and down in the hall. He looked up as soon as he saw them and said, 'Thank God you are back! Jeremy, Rachel, a terrible thing has happened. We must leave now. This instant.'

'Why? What's happened?' Jeremy asked.

'My wife, Marina called. She says the police are crawling all over Tinios – our semi private island. They seem to be under some delusion that my brother - Stanley, killed his wife! To make things worse, his wife has actually disappeared, gone missing. Marina fears that they might arrest him any moment now, on a cooked-up murder charge. You both must come with me. We must help him.'

Rachel asked wide eyed, 'Do we have time to pack?'

'Our seaplane leaves in forty-five minutes.'

Chapter Three

The next morning at Tinios, Lieutenant Ari Demakis was pacing up and down on the large sun speckled wooden patio, attached to the main living room of the Papanos beach house. Demakis was a tall and thin man with a serious face, tussled brown hair, a trimmed moustache and intense dark eyes that gave the peculiar impression that he could see beyond the realms of the ordinary man. At the moment, the eyes were taking in the surroundings and the panoramic view from the patio, which overlooked the leafy wooded path leading down to the private dock of the estate on Tinios. The spot offered a view of the entire island nestled like an emerald in the jewelled sapphire of the Aegean Sea.

The sheer beauty of the place momentarily managed to distract him from the task at hand. With some effort, he brought his mind back to the present. Upon his orders, his team was conducting a thorough search of the Papanos Estate. Reports of foul play on the estate had been seeping in through various sources over the past few days, and one informant had categorically told the authorities that a murder had been planned and executed by the influential Papanos family on their private island estate. They had gone as far as to say, that owing to the family's connections and enormous wealth, they would probably never be brought to book in a place like Greece.

These murmurs and loose talk had infuriated Ari Demakis. Born to a humble school teacher father and a mother who worked as a seamstress in an impoverished district of Athens, Ari had been a gifted student and his father had hoped that he would go on to study medicine. But funds were scarce and as soon as Ari's basic education was complete, he had chosen to join the Hellenic Gendarmerie at the tender age of seventeen. He had worked his way up the ranks through sheer hard work, determination and his penchant for cracking difficult cases. Over the years, he had earned quite a reputation for being very intelligent and above all - incorruptible, which by itself was a tremendous badge of honour in this part of the world. Now in his early forties, after having clocked close to twenty-five years on the force, he was not about to accept that justice was blinded by wealth and position. As far as he was concerned, if there was foul play involved, even the Gods would be brought to task if they fell under his jurisdiction!

A young gendarme came running up the path, almost breathless with excitement. He stopped to swallow a few mouthfuls of air, before hollering up to Demakis, 'Sir, we found something. A piece of ripped cloth and blood spatters in the boathouse below.'

'How convenient!' Ari said quietly to himself, as his lanky form plodded down the stairs from the patio.

An hour later he was back at the main house, interrogating Stanley Papanos in the study. The same young gendarme was standing by taking notes.

Demakis addressed Stanley in his no-nonsense way, 'Do you recognise this? We think it may be a part of your wife's nightgown.' He handed the scrap of ivory cotton trimmed with lace across to Stanley.

Stanley stuttered, 'I...I'm not sure. One nightgown looks the same as another to me.'

'Seen quite a few, have you?'

'I'm sure I don't know what you mean.'

'Come now, Sir. We are all men of the world here. I have been reading up on you, over the past few days. Press clippings and so on. Your reputation precedes you. The tabloids seem to have labelled you as an international playboy. Your every move is monitored by the press, is it not? Madame Bilkis - the belly dancer on the Papanos yacht, Madame Maria - the French actress in Paris, Susan Rivers - the American Ambassador's daughter, among others. The list is quite exhausting,' Demakis said, as the young gendarme who was taking notes, stopped to listen with his mouth open in astonishment. The pencil dropped from his grip and rolled towards Stanley Papanos.

Stanley spoke, as he bent down to retrieve the pencil that had come to a rolling stop near his foot, 'Stop it, Lieutenant Demakis. Please! With all due respect, I don't like your insinuations. And no, for your information, the press has got it all wrong as usual. Those women were mere acquaintances. And whatever links you may have come across were all prior to my marriage. I was very much in love with my wife. Fact of the matter is, that I was so besotted with her that I married her against the wishes of my family.'

'Was?'

'What?'

Demakis clarified, 'You said "was" when you referred to your wife just now. Now that is very interesting.'

'Merely a slip of the tongue. We were referring to incidents from the past. Anyhow, getting back to your questions, I meant to inform you that my wife and I had quarrelled shortly before she disappeared.'

'We'll come back to the quarrel later. Coming back to this piece of evidence, you say, you cannot positively identify this as belonging to your wife.' Then turning to the gendarme, he said, 'Georgas, keep taking notes.'

'Yes, Sir.' The young Georgas said, as he took the pencil back sheepishly from Stanley's outstretched hand.

Stanley answered, 'No, I cannot. Her maid will probably be better at identifying this...this piece of cloth, if it did indeed belong to my wife.'

'Alright. Now coming back to the quarrel and her "disappearance". Can you tell me exactly what happened?'

'Yes. It was on the afternoon just before the storm.'

'That would make it last Friday?'

'Yes.'

'Late that afternoon, I went to Ariana's room. I remember it was oppressively hot and humid and very quiet. Even the sea was quiet. Uncannily so.'

'Ah yes, the lull before the storm.'

'You could say that. I had a terrible headache. I wanted to borrow the balm that she uses. While I was talking to her, I noticed bruises on her left arm and asked her where she had gotten them from. She gave me some cock and bull story of having been at the village that morning. She said she slipped on the stone steps in the village.'

'You did not believe her. Why?'

'Because the bruises looked as though they were made by a man's hands – the spacing indicated a large thumb and two fingers. I am not as big a fool as you make me out to be, Lieutenant!'

'Go on.'

'For a while now, I had been watching her closely.'

'Why?'

'A sixth sense, I suppose. And then there were those letters warning me about my wife's alleged infidelity.'

'Who were they from?'

'I don't know. They weren't signed but they were all hand delivered, so it must have been someone from the village. They were written in Greek and they all said the same thing, in a crude roundabout way.'

'I see. How curious. Anonymous letters? Do you have them? I'd like to see them.'

'I'm afraid I crumpled them as soon as I got them and threw them away. You see, even apart from those damned letters, I was quite convinced that she was having an affair.'

'With someone in the village? Was the anonymous letter writer kind enough to mention with whom she was having an affair?' Demakis asked sarcastically.

'Yes. Local chap called Nikos Karalis. He runs a dry goods store in the village. His late father, Spiros, used to be our estate manager here in my father's time. My father and Spiros go back a long away. Apparently, Spiros and my father were at school together and while my father went up in the world, poor Spiros' fortunes spiralled down. According to our Grandmother, Spiros arrived here thirty-five years ago with his wife, both threadbare and penniless. He begged my father for a job, any job. The long and short of it is, that after a year or so on this island, as our estate manager, Spiros died quite suddenly when we were very young. And after his death, my father gifted his widow – Zaida, a house in the village, set her up with a lifelong pension and provided their boy with an education in Athens. She died in relative comfort a few years ago – all thanks to my father's magnanimity. And this is how her son repays our family's generosity. If you ask me, you ought to be questioning Nikos regarding my wife's whereabouts!'

'Right, Mr. Papanos. Thank you for letting us know about this. I will personally question this Mr. Nikos er...'

'Nikos Karalis, Sir.' Georgas filled in, reading from his notes.

'Yes, thank you, Georgas. This Mr. Nikos Karalis. I'll be sure to question him soon.'

'Good.'

'Please go on. What happened after the quarrel?'

'Nothing. That's just it. We quarrelled, I left her room and I haven't set eyes on her since. I just assumed that after the vicious things we said to each other, she had decided to leave me for good.'

'I see. That was last Friday. And you didn't think of looking for her or even filing a missing person's report?'

'No. I'm afraid I didn't. If she had gone off somewhere with her lover, I didn't want to make a public spectacle over a very private business. You yourself mentioned how the press goes to town the moment a drop of gossip about this family comes their way. I wanted to spare my family and myself the horror of a full-fledged newspaper scandal.'

'I can understand that but what I cannot come to terms with is this - for a man who claims to have been in love with his wife, rather, "besotted" with her, as you put it, you seem far more concerned about avoiding a newspaper scandal rather than exhibiting any concern whatsoever, over your own wife's welfare.'

'As I mentioned, I didn't think she would be in any danger. If anything has in fact happened to her then Nikos is the chap you want, not me.'

'I see. And I will question him too. We're just beginning our investigation. We are anyway going to question everybody on the island. Meanwhile if I were you, I wouldn't go anywhere without informing the Gendarmerie.'

Chapter Four

While Ari Demakis was questioning Stanley Papanos in the study, Rachel was seated in the living room sipping sugary Tsai or herbal tea and listening to Marina's rendition of the events over the past week. Marina's black and white tabby, affectionately named Moussaka was curled up beside her. Aristea Papanos was dozing in an armchair by the window. It was a hot day and she looked her age - frail and tired. Jeremy and Stavros had left them a few minutes ago, to walk down to the docks and see what the police had found thus far.

Stavros' wife - Marina Papanos was in her forties and while she had individually good features, something in the way they came together on her face, along with a slightly longish Greek nose, prevented her from being considered a classical beauty. As she spoke loudly in a harsh voice, Rachel thought she reminded her of an animated crow, crowing away.

'I knew that girl Ariana was going to be trouble, as soon as I set eyes on her! Didn't I say so, Grandmamma?' As Marina spoke, Moussaka - the cat, raised her head to see what had agitated her human and then yawned and went back to sleep.

Aristea came out of her comfortable nap and nodded at her, 'Yes, but you say that about most women you meet. Nothing but trouble, you say. But I must say Ariana was a quiet sort. So shy and yielding. Quiet as a mouse. One never knew when she was in the house'

'And I always say, the quiet ones are the ones to watch out for. What with all that cunning and scheming going on in their heads. Good girls are talkative because they have clean hearts and nothing to hide. Like me.' Miranda said the last bit with a thump to her chest and the Greek flourish for the dramatic. Moussaka jumped up and then with a disdainful look of reproach at them all for disturbing her slumber again, the cat left the room through the window, to look for quieter environs.

'Hmm. But I must admit, Ariana was very different from Stanley's other girls. At any rate, she was a great improvement on the last one. What was her name...? Ah yes, Bilkis, the belly dancer.' Aristea smiled before closing her eyes again as Marina's tirade started again.

'Stanley and his women! Didn't Madame Zorba say that he'll bring misfortune upon the family some day? And now look at us. The police crawling all over our estate. Disgraceful!'

The door opened halfway and the maid - Nerissa popped her head in and yelled at someone outside, 'They're over here.'

Marina shouted, 'How many times have I told you not to shout like a peasant, Nerissa! Can't you see we have company!'

Nerissa shrugged her shoulders and brought her voice down a notch, 'That Madame Zorba walked up from the village. She says she is looking for you.'

The door was pushed open completely by a short and portly woman with rosy cheeks, wearing a shapeless print dress made of coarse local cotton. She had a red scarf tied over her head and spoke in a loud cheerful voice, 'And so I am! Go away Nerissa and bring me some tea. Oh, Aristea I am so, so sorry to hear about Ariana and that dear child, Stanley... oh, I didn't know you had guests.'

Rachel couldn't help but smile at her.

Marina made introductions. 'This is Madame Zorba. She is our grand aunt, and a well-known fortune teller in these parts.'

Madame Zorba harrumphed, 'Is that all you can say? I am not just a well-known fortune teller but a great one! My family has had the gift of the third sight for many generations. Of course, it skipped my sister, Aristea. Only I have the gift in our generation. One of our ancestors was indeed none other than one of the chosen Oracles at Delphi - the high priestess, Pythia!'

Rachel spoke, 'Oh my! How fascinating! But surely you mean second sight. Do you use a crystal ball?'

'Crystal ball? What nonsense! Who needs a tawdry crystal ball when one has the natural gift of the mighty Oracle? The third eye! Far supercedes the second sight. Hence, I call it the third sight. My sister here, is the one who collects crystals. Heliotropes, tourmalines, amethysts, carnelians, Burmese sapphires and rubies, and that fancy one that fell out of the sky. What do you call that again?'

Aristea spoke up, 'I think you are referring to the Agni Mani.' Turning to Rachel, she explained further, 'It is a Sanskrit word which means the fire pearl. My son brought it back from a sea voyage to Java. The Javanese natives told him that it is the stone of the Gods that fell from the sky. It is said that whoever possesses it, gains mastery over the senses and is helped by a divine hand in this world. Our fortunes certainly changed for the better once it arrived. My son believed that the success of the Papanos shipping empire was a direct result of owning the fire pearl. And since it is very rare and sought after for its mythical properties, it is priceless.'

'That is an incredible story. Is this fire pearl a meteorite of some sort?'

'We believe it is referred to as a tektite in scientific circles, an object formed in the atmosphere millions of years ago in a cosmic collision. It is the prize of our collection with a value far above rubies.'

Rachel looked at her and said, 'How splendid. I've never seen one. You must show me your crystal collection.'

Before Aristea could reply, Madame Zorba brought the conversation back to herself by interjecting, 'You would be disappointed. It is a black and pitted stone and isn't much to look at, whatever the legends around it claim. The crystals, on the other hand are quite beautiful. Pretty baubles as they are, I personally don't need their help. Oh, I can see into nether worlds, a place where others in my profession fear to tread.'

Aristea spoke up wearily, 'Yes, yes, your stories have fascinated many people into parting with their money.'

Madame Zorba gave her a withering look. 'And didn't I tell you that as we grew older, you - my own sister, would become jealous of my gifts and turn into a traitor, Aristea.'

Aristea responded, 'I merely want to prevent one of our unsuspecting guests from believing your prophecies of doom and gloom. You have scared away enough of my friends in the past, my dear.'

Rachel spoke laughingly, 'Oh, I don't mind at all. Won't you tell me what's in store for me?'

Madame Zorba spoke, 'Marina, go and see what's taking Nerissa so long. I've had a long tiring walk and I want my tea.'

Marina grumbled, 'It's only been two minutes.' But she got up and left the room.

As the door closed behind Marina, Madame Zorba came and sat next to Rachel on the sofa and said, 'Mind! I only tell what I see and if I see something bad, I shall tell you that as well. Now, show me your palm. No, no, not your right hand, for women, it is always the left!'

Rachel meekly withdrew her right hand and extended her left palm. As Madame Zorba scrutinised Rachel's palm, Aristea shrugged her shoulders and reclined in her easy chair once more. With closed eyes and a smile, she said, 'Don't tell me later that I didn't warn you, Rachel.'

Rachel smiled back, 'I promise I shan't.'

After a few moments of pin drop silence, Madame Zorba said, 'Ah, yes, you have courage, great courage...it has been tested many times already and you are married, are you not?'

'Yes, I am.' Rachel replied.

'Yes, you are married to a good man. He is much older than you. I see a big, old stone house in a cold, cold country far away.' Then she shuddered, 'But you are foolhardy to have ever come here. And a child, I see a child…and I see a great sorrow will befall you, if you don't leave this island immediately…and I see hovering around the child a black cloud…oh, yes, a black cloud of…'

Aristea spoke up tonelessly, 'Death. I bet she sees death. She always does.'

Madame Zorba flung Rachel's hand away and stood up. 'I shall not stay here and be insulted. I am leaving. My great powers have never lied before, Aristea. Did I not warn you about Kosta and Delphine's flight? And about Spiros' death? And didn't I tell you that I foresaw Stanley's downfall? I see you still scoff at me. When Stanley stands behind bars after he is arrested, perhaps you will remember my gift.'

Aristea rose up in her chair with a sudden agility that belied her age and spoke angrily, 'Oh get out, Althea! You and your gift be damned! All mumbo jumbo and nothing else. How dare you come to my house to gloat over my grandson's misfortune. Leave now!'

'I am leaving!' Then turning to Rachel, she said, 'And you should leave too. There is nothing but sorrow for you here. Leave at once! Go back home as soon as possible.'

Aristea said wearily to her sister, the fire seemed to have gone out of her suddenly, 'I wish you'd take your own advice!'

Althea Zorba looked at Aristea angrily before walking towards the door and leaving the room without saying another word.

Rachel spoke up hesitatingly, 'But Aristea, she was right about my husband being older than me and I think she described our home - Rutherford Hall, back in England, perfectly.'

'Really Rachel, don't take her nonsense seriously. You are very young. Even in this modern day and age, most husbands are older than their wives. And with your British accent, even I could have told you that you have a house in a cold country! And I don't claim to possess any second or third sight. I am perfectly happy that my normal eyesight is as good as it is, at my age!'

Rachel smiled, 'Yes, you're probably right. She was a bit off about a child. We don't have one. Well, I suppose she could have been talking about Toby – our dog. He is like a child to me. I've left him in my mother's care. I do hope he's alright. Perhaps I ought to call home and check on him.'

'Of course your dog will be alright,' Aristea said with an incredulous look. 'And don't you get taken in by all that talk about death. She's been predicting my death every single year without fail, for the past ten years and look, I'm still around. Like a creaking gate, I shall probably go on for years! Just to defy her, if I can. Third sight, my foot!'

Rachel laughed out loud. 'Well that certainly makes me feel better!' But behind her outwardly cheerful façade, she had to admit to herself that she was mildly disturbed by the fortune teller's dire warning. She made up her mind to call her mother and check on Toby later in the day.

Chapter Five

Jeremy was addressing Stavros and Rachel in the living room. 'Well, this is serious. Lieutenant Demakis means business. So far, the inquiry was simply for a missing person. That too based on local gossip and hearsay. With the new evidence of blood splatters, and that piece of cloth, chances are that it will now become a full-fledged criminal investigation.'

Aristea spoke up from her seat, near the window, 'But how can they? They haven't found a body yet.'

Jeremy responded. 'Signs of violence such as blood splatters are enough for police to launch a criminal investigation, especially if the forensics come back with the report that the blood found is human.'

Aristea spoke, 'I see and then what happens?'

'I'm afraid I don't know much about Greek police procedure but back in England, the spouse usually comes under suspicion and if evidence of recent disharmony can be proven in the marriage, an arrest is usually made.'

'So, will they arrest Stanley?'

'It's not likely at this point but if they do, bail will probably be granted unless they can furnish further conclusive evidence.'

'Like a body?'

'That or a witness or witnesses.'

'What if they find neither?'

'Then the investigation will be made through interrogations of the people that the victim knew, or those in her vicinity.'

'And if that brings up nothing? Will the investigation be closed eventually? There are so many unsolved cases that one hears about.'

Jeremy looked at her shrewdly and said, 'Yes, but despite popular belief, those are extremely rare and I get the feeling that Ari Demakis is not a man who has many unsolved cases to his credit. I don't know what you know about this alleged crime, Aristea but if you do know something I would suggest you make a clean breast of it. A great many people underestimate the tenacity of the police force, to their own detriment.'

'What would a frail old woman like me know about crime? I was merely curious about what they would do to Stanley, if nothing further was found.'

Rachel spoke up, 'I am sure Jeremy never meant to suggest that you had anything to do with this crime, if indeed one was committed. However, there may be something you can remember from the night in question, which may have seemed trivial at the time, yet may have a significant bearing on Ariana's disappearance.'

'Well, if there is, my memory fails me. One of the things about getting old is how you British say, I seem to be losing my marbles slowly but surely.'

A female voice with a thick Arabic accent rang out from the entrance of the room, 'I know nobody who has their marbles more intact, Madame Papanos! Or should I call you Aristea for old time's sake, and darling Stavros, so good to see you again...'

As they all turned to look, a gorgeous woman with red and golden hair, that fell in luxuriant waves to her waist, appeared. She was wearing a bright smile and a flame coloured skin-tight dress, which accentuated her voluptuous curves and left little to the imagination.

The awkward pin drop silence which ensued, ended a moment later, as Stavros stood up and exclaimed, 'Good heavens, Bilkis! What are you doing here?'

Bilkis Hamadi strode into the room with the grace of a panther and answered Stavros with some amusement, 'That's a fine way to greet an old friend! Aren't you going to introduce me to your friends?' She moved forward and kissed him loudly on both cheeks, even as her eyes were fixed seductively on Jeremy.

Stavros stuttered, 'Yes, yes, of course, where are my manners? Allow me to introduce Madam Bilkis Hamadi, one of the finest and if I may say so, among the most famous belly dancers in the world and Bilkis, you already know Grandmamma and Marina. And these are my friends – Jeremy Richards and his wife, Rachel. They are visiting us from England. Jeremy and I go back a long way. We were at Oxford together.'

Jeremy nodded and held out his hand, 'Charmed I'm sure.'

Rachel piped up, 'Indeed. I've never met a belly dancer before.'

Bilkis gave her a strange look and Rachel smiled and raised an eyebrow, as Bilkis ignored her completely and hugged Jeremy with greater vigour than she did Stavros. And then proceeded to kiss him on both cheeks. Bilkis said, looking meaningfully into Jeremy's eyes, 'And that is how we Egyptians greet new friends that we want to know better.'

Aristea spoke up, her voice hoarse, 'That's all very well. But what are you doing here? I thought you had gone back to Cairo for good!'

Bilkis let go of her hold on Jeremy, 'Oh! It is a long story. I cannot possibly tell it with such a parched throat. Darling Stavros, be a good jinn and get me a drink. The stronger the better.'

Stavros got up and Aristea's voice shot out, 'Sit down, Stavros. I'll tell Nerissa to bring her tea. Now tell me, what brings you to our island.'

Bilkis shrugged and sat down on a couch. 'I had a performance at Athens and then Patra, and later we set sail on my friend – Tom Preston's new yacht but that horrible storm took us off our course and then I remembered your island was close by and we anchored for safety, at the hidden cove on the other side.'

Jeremy asked, 'Do you mean to say you've been anchored here for over a week now?' Jeremy and Rachel exchanged a glance, as they both realised that Bilkis Hamadi would have been on the island, close to the time Ariana disappeared.

'Yes, we arrived last Friday, quite late in the night, at around nine or ten PM. And good that we docked the yacht safely in the hidden cove, when we did. That storm lasted two days! We were supposed to leave once the weather cleared up but Tom found it so charming. I told him about the hidden caves near the cliffs and he really loves to explore new places. He's a geologist, you know and he finds rocks and caves interesting. He found another underwater cave, the first day he went exploring. He says some of the caves here are sure to go very deep. And that this entire island is probably built on a labyrinth of subterranean tunnels and caves. He thinks they could go back to the Neolithic period or something like that. He wanted to see more and continue his little explorations, and I spent my days swimming and sunbathing. So, we stayed a few more days.'

'Fascinating story.' Marina said sarcastically.

Bilkis ignored her and continued, 'We were finally going to set sail today. We stocked up at the Karalis dry goods store this morning but the police came to the store, while we were there and were asking all sorts of questions.' Her eyes were as large as saucers, as she said in a hushed voice, 'They asked us not to leave the island. It seems that there is a rumour that Stanley's wife is missing. Possibly even murdered!' Then with a shrug, her voice came back to its normal octave, as she said, 'Well, I wouldn't be surprised if he did bump off that insipid little creature he got married to! Boredom in a marriage can be so tiresome, worse than death, don't you agree?' She said with feeling, directing her gaze at Stavros this time.

Marina spoke in a sweet voice, laced with venom, 'Oh, we married people get by. But it always amuses me to see that unmarried women usually have such wisdom when it comes to such matters…'

Bilkis retorted with a sly smile. 'That is why we stay unmarried, is it not?' Then looking directly at Marina, she spoke in a low melodious voice,

'But marriage is not the only thing, is it Marina? Such a tragedy that you could not bear any children. But I agree with you partially. You know what I find? I find that barren women can sometimes become very bitter, especially once they cross forty. The clock ticks in desperation, no? I am sure you would agree, er ah Mrs...' she said glancing at Rachel.

'Call me Rachel. I'm afraid I can't contribute to this, ahem, interesting conversation. It would be rather presumptuous on my part, were I to profess the kind of wisdom that mature ladies as yourself possess,' Rachel responded tongue-in-cheek, inwardly taken aback by the open animosity displayed by the two women.

Marina lounged back and stared at her crimson nails, as she casually addressed Bilkis, 'Barren? Me? What about you? It is such a joke, words like this coming from a woman who every man will bed, yet no one will wed. And now you are past your prime, surely inching towards forty yourself. Sadly, all that makeup does not conceal the lines around your eyes. I feel for you, I really do. A dwindling career, no husband, no child...'

Stavros looked distressed, 'I say, there is really no need for...'

Bilkis threw her head back and laughed. 'My dear, you are misinformed. My career has never been better and hence unlike most women, I have never needed a husband as a meal ticket. And I have a beautiful five-year-old daughter, Samara. She really is beautiful. Sometimes she does not look like my daughter at all. As though she doesn't have a drop of Egyptian blood in her. Strange how some children can look so little like their mothers and yet have the same heart.'

Stavros looked astonished, 'I am happy for you. I had no idea. Where is your daughter now?'

'On the boat with Tom, as we speak. I thought you all knew about her. Didn't Aristea tell you that I was with child? After all, she met me last when I was pregnant, about six years ago, didn't you, Aristea?'

Aristea spoke up with steel in her voice, 'We are not in the habit of discussing the private lives of performers and dancers at our family dinner table. I hope you will excuse me, I have had a long day. Stavros, be kind enough to show Miss Hamadi out. I am sure she is anxious to return to her child.'

Despite Aristea's surprising rudeness, Bilkis got up gracefully, 'There is no need for such formality between old friends. As you know, Madame Papanos, I know my way around this house quite well. I can show myself out. But I should like to meet Stanley before I leave.'

Aristea replied coldly, 'That will not be possible, I'm afraid.'

Stavros spoke kindly, 'Perhaps another time, Bilkis. As you are aware, he is in the middle of this, this terrible situation...'

A laconic voice came from the door, 'Who is in the middle of a terrible situation?'

Rachel turned to see Stanley Papanos standing in the doorway. As his eyes fell on Bilkis, she noticed that the colour drained from his face.

Chapter Six

At dinner that night, the family was quiet. Rachel tried to keep a conversation going but soon realised that she was the only one participating; with Stavros and Jeremy responding intermittently, out of politeness. She was about to give it up as a bad job when they all heard a crash from the next room.

As Stavros got up to investigate, Dorkas the maid came in with dessert and told him that it was just the cat. It had broken a vase in the next room, in its attempt to climb out of the window.

Stavros sat back down and spoke accusingly, 'Marina, you are overfeeding that cat again and now it can't even move about without breaking things.'

Marina responded, 'Don't blame me. It is Grandmamma – she's the one who is always feeding her.'

Aristea shrugged, 'Moussaka never had a good sense of balance, even when she came here as a kitten. Whoever said cats always land on their feet, evidently never met her!'

Rachel laughed. 'I think Moussaka is perfectly charming. She paid us a visit in the guest cottage when we were dressing for dinner.'

Stavros spoke, 'Please be careful while petting her. Apart from being grossly overweight and having no sense of balance, she is quite temperamental as well. She can give people nasty scratches. Marina got a nasty wound on her forearm just last week. She had to put bandages on it.'

Marina nodded, 'I don't know why I put up with that cat but she can be quite sweet now and then and make up for all her transgressions. I hope you haven't been stupid enough to keep a cat, Rachel.'

As the conversation turned towards the more cheerful topic of pets, the atmosphere of the room changed. Jeremy related their own amusing story of how they had found and adopted Toby. As laughter returned to the room, Rachel found it interesting that simply talking about pets, was enough to bring most people out of the darkest of moods.

Later, Jeremy and Rachel decided to take a post prandial stroll on the beach below the house. The moon was shimmering over the Aegean Sea as far as the eye could see. They could see the lights on the island of Lefkada, in the distance. The stars were out in their full glory. From where they were, they could see lanterns hung over balustrades and doors in the village above them; giving a warm, gentle light to illuminate the night. While the smell of the salty sea air filled their lungs with freshness, the sound of the waves and a large quantity of delicious Greek food that they had partaken, lulled them into a state of deep peace and contentment.

Jeremy took her hand in his, as they walked.

Rachel spoke first, 'It is so beautiful here. Everything around us seems as though it's all touched by enchantment somehow. This is exactly how I imagined paradise must be when I was a child.'

'Quite right. Hard to imagine a place like this could become a stage for any crime, let alone a violent one. But then I've always known that the human mind is a strange thing. It can become blasé to great beauty in no time. Even beauty as magical as this. The locals probably don't even notice it anymore. We all tend to take so much in our lives for granted.'

Rachel smiled, 'I quite agree. Take me, for instance, it's appalling how I take you for granted most of the time.'

Jeremy's eyes twinkled. 'Yes. Quite appalling. We need to fix that or I might just be whisked away by Egyptian belly dancers.'

Rachel grinned. 'Not unless we want another violent crime committed on this island, darling.

And coming to that, I'm not sure if there has been a crime at all. What if Ariana simply disappeared with her lover, as Stanley assumed. It's only been a week. What if she went off in a huff somewhere or she's just taking some time off. We'd all look like perfect fools, if he gets a postcard from her, one of these days.'

'I've considered that but there are those blood spatters. And the night she disappeared, she couldn't have possibly gotten off of this island, in such severe storm conditions. I get the sense that there is the distinct possibility that she could be lying murdered somewhere.'

'Hmm...I think that tomorrow, we ought to do a spot of exploring, ourselves. Those caves that Bilkis was talking about, sound terribly interesting. Strange that no one in the family told us of their existence.'

'I'm not the least bit surprised, darling. With all that's been going on, informing us about the local tourist attractions was probably the last thing on their minds.'

'Jeremy! If your wife went missing on an island which has underground cavern systems, I should think that would be the first place you would start your search for a missing person.'

'Yes, I see what you are driving at. Good God! How could I have overlooked that? I wonder if the police are aware.'

Rachel shrugged, 'It's quite possible that the locals would have told them, but then again we can't be sure.'

'We ought to inform Lieutenant Demakis and perhaps get a few of the locals to form a search party, together with the police.'

'Yes. Though God knows what we'll find in there.'

'Or if we'll find anything at all.'

'Hmm, you know Jeremy, there is something else.'

'Go on.'

'Perhaps it's nothing. I may be imagining it but don't you think, there was something very strange about the way that Aristea and Marina were treating Bilkis. Almost as though their meanness towards her was exaggerated and magnified, to steer the conversation and our attention away from her disclosure about the caves.'

'Or, there seems to be some sort of history there. Stanley looked positively green about the gills when he spotted that Bilkis woman, and she isn't all that unpleasant to look at.'

Rachel smiled, 'Yes, I noticed that too. She is quite the femme fatale. But somehow, contrary to popular belief, I always feel that women like her can become quite easily victimised by rich and powerful people. There is something about the way Aristea practically shooed her away, right after Stanley appeared. As though she didn't want any conversation between them. And strange how Stanley just took to his room after the incident, like a sulking twelve-year-old boy.'

'Yes, he's a strange sort of cove. Nothing like Stavros.'

'I've never seen two brothers more unlike each other! Chalk and cheese springs to mind. Are you quite sure they are related by blood?'

'Oh, yes, positively. Their father-Kosta was Greek and their mother–Delphine was British. While Stavros looks exactly like his father, Stanley has obviously taken after the mother.'

'Did you ever meet the parents?'

'I met the father once, at Oxford - the legendary Kostakis Papanos. He was a most interesting chap. Took us out to dinner at the Savoy and regaled us with the most interesting anecdotes throughout.'

'What sort of anecdotes?'

'Oh this and that, mostly on how he set up his shipping empire from scratch. And there was the amusing story, as to how he met his wife, Delphine and married her.'

'Do tell me!'

'Apparently, he had taken some German business partners to the temple at Delphi, as a tourist outing after their business meeting was successfully concluded. And there was this young British woman who was travelling with her aunt and she mistook him to be a Greek guide. He played along all day. The next morning, they returned to Delphi. He had managed to ditch the aunt somehow and taken her out on her own, to show her the woods behind Delphi. They spent the entire afternoon hiking through the woods. She told him that she was named Delphine after Delphi and that it was almost like a pilgrimage for her, to finally visit Delphi. He said they had an incredible chemistry, unlike anything he had felt with any woman before. He said he made her laugh. To cut a long story short, they ended up making love in the woods and he proposed marriage to her, by the end of the day.

She told him that she had fallen in love with him too but sadly she couldn't marry him. He asked if she had refused him because he was a penniless guide. And she told him that money had nothing to do with it. She could support them both. It seems she had some money of her own but that after her parents died, her aunt had control of it and if she married without her consent, she would not have access to her inheritance. And her aunt was old school; she would never allow her to marry a Greek. So, they would have to wait till she was twenty-five. He pretended to be devastated and let her go. She and her aunt went off to Santorini for a week.

A week later, once she was back at Athens with her aunt in tow, he surprised them both by upgrading them to the Presidential suite at their hotel and twelve dozen roses, strewn around the suite.'

'Oh goodness, they are romantic, these Greek men.'

'To cut a long story short, he finally revealed his real identity as one of the richest men in Greece and wooed her and the aunt until they both said yes. Of course, the fact that he was rich as Croesus must have had something to do with the aunt's change of heart, about her niece marrying a Greek.'

'Oh, don't be so cynical, darling. It all sounds terribly romantic to me.'

'Apparently it was. By all accounts they had a very happy marriage.'

'How did they die?'

'Their sea plane crashed near the coast of Patra about six years ago, killing all on board – the pilot and five passengers.'

'Truly a Greek tragedy. How sad.'

'Quite. But at least they were together, even in death.'

'Why, Jeremy Richards, you surprise me! You are quite the romantic yourself!'

Jeremy grinned back at her, 'Goodness! Must watch my step. Probably something in the air here.'

'I'd rather you didn't,' Rachel said, looking up at him with a coquettish smile.

'Your wish is my command, milady!' Jeremy laughed and gathered her up in his arms, kissing her soundly.

Chapter Seven

The next morning, Jeremy and Rachel were walking on the path that led from the guest cottage to the main house, for breakfast. The path was partially covered by a trellis with a profusion of scarlet bougainvillaea growing abundantly. Where the path forked, they took a right, which would take them right up to the main house. The left fork meandered down to a wooden pier and the whitewashed steps leading to the private beach. The view was stunning from there and the bright scarlet flowers seemed to frame the Aegean Sea.

'There's nothing quite like a morning in Greece. Just look at the sea today! It's glowing like a pale turquoise jewel. I've never seen anything quite as beautiful darling, have you?'

Jeremy looked distracted. He looked towards the sea and replied, 'Yes darling, I was thinking that we ought to go down to the village, as soon as we're done with our breakfast and have a word with Nikos Karalis, and also try and catch up with Tom-whatever-his-name-is, Bilkis' boyfriend on the boat. He's been exploring and may be of some help in the search...'

Before he could finish, they heard a commotion, and as the house came into view, they could see that Stanley Papanos was being led away by a gendarme. Nerissa followed them, sniffling into a handkerchief. Ari Demakis was talking to Stavros and Marina. The latter looked animated.

'What's going on here?' Jeremy asked, as they reached within earshot of the group.

Marina spoke, 'They've made an arrest. Finally!'

Demakis added, 'My gendarmes made a search of the Karalis dry goods store last night. They discovered a bag with Ariana Papanos' personal items - some pieces of jewellery and her wedding ring, hidden in a jute sack filled with walnuts.'

'So, why have you arrested Stanley?' Rachel asked puzzled.

'Madame, we arrested Nikos Karalis last night. Mr. Stanley Papanos is merely being escorted to identify his wife's things. Nerissa - the maid has also been asked to confirm if those items belonged to her mistress. We also found a torn shirt with blood stains on the cuffs in the bag. We think it belongs to Karalis.'

Jeremy spoke, 'Would you mind awfully, if we were to question Mr. Karalis?'

Ari Demakis smiled, 'Be my guest. Mr. Stavros has informed me of your tenure with the Scotland Yard. Also, that you and Madame are private detectives of some repute in England. It would be interesting for me to see what conclusion you draw in your interrogation. He is currently in the local village lock up. Please don't expect British standards, as there is no police station on this island. We are lucky that we have an old, two-room jail house in the village that houses drunk and disorderly locals, from time to time.'

Jeremy nodded, 'That is most gracious of you, Lieutenant Demakis. And by the way, most of our smaller English villages too have no police stations.'

Rachel added with a grin, 'That is true. In one of the cases we solved back in England, the police had to contain a suspect in a meat locker of a large house.'

Ari nodded, 'Come with me, then.'

As breakfast was forgotten, Jeremy and Rachel followed Demakis, as he led the way into the picturesque village.

Ten minutes later, they were face to face with Nikos Karalis.

He was shouting in Greek at the gendarme in front of him.

Rachel asked Demakis, 'What's he saying? Does he speak any English?'

Before Demakis could answer, Nikos looked at her and said, 'I'm calling them stupid idiots! I am a decorated war hero. They can't treat me like this. Anyone could have put those things in my store. It's open all day! Half the time there's no one to mind it. Who the devil are you?'

Demakis intervened and introduced Jeremy and Rachel to Karalis.

Rachel said, 'We are here to help you. Tell us what you know, Mr. Karalis.'

Nikos looked dejected. 'What's the point? These oafs have made up their minds that I've killed Ariana and hidden her body somewhere.'

Jeremy said, 'Can we start from the beginning, please. Did you meet Ariana on the day that she disappeared? According to her husband, you both were having an affair.'

'He's an idiot too. Ariana was very unhappy in her marriage and we were friends. Sure, she came to me from time to time for comfort. I've known her since my student days in Athens. I met her in 1939. She had just turned eighteen and was working as a waitress in a hotel, very close to my university.'

'Was she your girlfriend, back in your student days?' Rachel asked, following a hunch.

'Yes, we were in love. I wanted to marry her before I joined the army in 1940. I fought in the Greco-Italian war, along with most of the boys from the university. Just before we left to fight, I brought her here to the island, to meet my mother and before the week was over, she met that oaf Stanley and she chose him over me. He didn't even fight in the war,' Nikos spat in disgust.

'That must have made you angry,' Rachel said.

'Of course, I was angry. I wanted to wring her neck back then, but then my mother made me see sense. She told me I was better off without a woman who would choose money over love. And I realised that my mother was right. Although, every time I shot a fascist, I thought of her. Then I remembered that even in my university days, I caught her cheating on me with an older man but I forgave her and took her back. Then she went off with Stanley. I am glad I didn't get married to her. A very beautiful woman but a heart breaker. She has no sense of loyalty.'

'But you stayed on friendly terms with her.'

'I had no choice. This is a small island and we were bound to meet. She came down to my store often and stopped to talk. We took a few walks together as well.'

Demakis spoke, 'You are a very forgiving man, Mr. Karalis. Most men in your shoes would have wanted revenge.'

'Oh, I've have had my revenge. A month ago, she came begging to me, to take her back. She said that she regretted her decision to marry Stanley and wanted to get back with me. And I sent her packing. Told her that since I had been decorated as a war hero, I had higher standards now.' He smirked.

'And what was her reaction to your rejection?' Jeremy asked.

'She was furious. Hysterical. She threatened that she would destroy me.'

Rachel asked, 'And did you have any contact with her after that?'

'Yes. On the afternoon before the storm. She sent one of the servants from the house, a woman called Dorkas to the store, with a hysterical note saying that she was in terrible danger and that she desperately needed my help. In the note, she asked me to meet her near the hidden cove at three o'clock.'

'So, what happened?'

'I got delayed. As you know, we had a hurricane warning. Half the village had come by to stock up on provisions, in preparation for the hurricane. By the time I finished serving customers, it was about four o'clock and the storm was gathering. The sky was overcast. I closed the store and reached the hill above the cove, by about four twenty but there was no sign of her. I called out but there was no response from below, so I didn't bother to go all the way down.'

'Did you see anyone else about?'

'Yes, I saw a local boy, Dimitri, on the hills. He was still out with his goats and I told him to take his herd back home as the storm was coming.'

'Now think back carefully, did you see anyone else in the vicinity?'

'No. Not another soul. Most of the locals were in their homes by then.'

Demakis spoke, 'What about this note? Do you still have it?'

Nikos shook his head, 'I can't remember what I did with it. Perhaps it's still around in one of my pockets somewhere. You people are the experts when it comes to searching. If it is still there, your gendarmes should be able to find it. And Dorkas can confirm my story about the note.'

'Thank you, Mr. Karalis. We will question her too.'

Nikos spoke. 'Now I have a question for you. How long are you planning to keep me in this dump, Lieutenant?'

'Till we find out what really happened to Ariana Papanos. At the moment, the evidence is stacked against you and as you know, under Greek law, a man under suspicion is considered guilty until unless proven innocent.'

'I tell you I have no idea how her things ended up in my store!'

Demakis spoke, 'And what about your blood-stained shirt, Mr. Karalis? Are you going to claim even that was planted there to frame you? Your washer-woman has positively identified it as being one of your shirts.'

'It may be my shirt but I have no idea how blood got on to it, or why it was stashed in my store. Do you think I'd be stupid enough to keep it in my store, if I was guilty of this crime that you are accusing me of? I can think of a thousand better hiding places on this island!'

Rachel spoke, 'That reminds me, Mr. Karalis, one last question. We've just been made aware that there are caves in the vicinity of the hidden cove. Could she have taken refuge there? And from where you were standing, could you see the entrance to the cave?'

'No. That entrance is hidden behind a large group of boulders. And it is not visible from the beach let alone the top of the hill. The cliff juts over the boulders. I could only see a few fishing boats and the Papanos yacht anchored there. But I doubt she would go there, even to wait. Those caves are dark, dank and smelly and she is terrified of the dark.'

Jeremy spoke, 'Right. And while we're on the subject of caves, Lieutenant Demakis, my wife and were wondering if your men could get together a few of the locals and...'

Demakis responded before he could finish, 'Ah, there Mr. Richards, we are ahead of you. Two of my gendarmes have already got a search party ready this morning and are probably in the caves as we speak.'

Chapter Eight

'Tom Preston. Always happy to see a pretty face. C'mon up!' The large blonde man spoke with an American twang, as he extended his hand out to Rachel, and helped her step aboard the yacht. He had a sunburned face, a large red nose and cornflour blue eyes under the straw hat. He looked about forty-five-years old and was dressed casually in a white shirt, khaki shorts and canvas shoes.

Jeremy climbed on board right behind Rachel, smoothening down her pale blue chiffon dress, which had ballooned up in the breeze.

Rachel smiled back at Jeremy, embarrassed as she tried to control her flying dress with one hand and her hat with the other. Then turning to the man on board, she took his hand and said, 'Thank you,

Mr. Preston. I'm Rachel Markham and this is my husband, Jeremy Richards. We came by to see the caves and spotted you on board. What a marvellous yacht you have here!'

'Why, thank you. She is my pride and joy. A new acquisition. Bought her for a song from a fellow at Cairo. The war changed many fortunes, thankfully mine too!' He smiled, as he turned to shake Jeremy's extended hand.

Jeremy smiled and asked, 'What line of business are you in, Mr. Preston?'

'Oh, this and that. Mostly that...' he responded with a devilish grin and a twinkle in his eye.

'Interesting.' Jeremy said with a raised eyebrow.

Tom Preston spoke, 'To be honest, I'm just a lowly geologist by profession. I was working at Boston University in the Geology department. I came to Greece to collect some samples for the university. That was before I discovered that I had a long-lost uncle back in America and he's in oil. Poor old sod is rich as the devil and has no other kith or kin apart from yours truly. Fortune smiled upon me, as they say, and thanks to Uncle Richie, I gave up my dull and boring job at Boston University. And now, I've taken it upon myself to pursue several personal interests around the globe.'

Rachel smiled, 'Well, isn't that serendipitous for you.'

Tom nodded, 'Truly. Ever since old man Preston took a shine to me, it's been all hunky-dory!'

Jeremy spoke. 'Ah yes, the name does ring a bell. Do you mean that Richie Preston – the Texan oil millionaire, is your uncle? Well, who hasn't heard of him!'

Preston shrugged. 'What do you know? Truth is stranger than fiction, huh? Uncle Richie was the black sheep of the family on my father's side. My father's only brother. Got into a lot of trouble with the law in his younger days and my mother made my dad cut off all ties with him ages ago. But he made it big with the good 'ol rags to riches tale that the world knows about now, and I thought I'd meet up with him after my mother died, God bless her wicked little soul for coming between two brothers. And such a wonderful guy he turned out to be. Frankly, I've a lot more in common with him than I ever had with my own dad. Old Richie said the same thing himself. My dad died chained to a desk, spent his whole life working nine-to-five at a dull bank job in Boston, while I've always been a great one for living life on the edge. Danger and adventure – those are the things that turn me on.'

Jeremy raised an eyebrow, 'And geology was your choice of profession?'

Rachel gave him a sideways glance and changed the subject, 'By the way, one of our acquaintances – a Mr. Ira Pembrook is a professor of history at

Boston University. I must write him and tell him that I bumped into you in Greece.'

Preston nodded, 'That'll be nice, although I don't recall being on very friendly terms with Pembrook. Still, it's a small world, huh?'

Rachel grinned, 'It certainly is, Mr. Preston.'

'Call me Tom, please. Mr. Preston was my father.' Tom Preston told her with a mock pained expression on his face.

Rachel laughed, 'Well alright, Tom, Miss Hamadi did inform us that you've been helter-skelter exploring the caves around this island for the past week.'

'Did she now? That little sphinx sure gets about spinning stories behind my back, I can tell you! I've explored some, but what interests me more at the moment, is what you two Brits are doing here on this tiny island, far away from the fleshpots of Athens.'

He led them to the far side of the deck, where there was a large white umbrella, shading the seating arrangements on the deck.

Rachel made herself comfortable, as Jeremy sat back and explained how and why they were there.

Tom shook his head in disbelief. 'Private dicks huh, the two of you. I would've never guessed it, not in a million years! You Miss, look like you've just walked over from the Ascot and your husband, well, he just looks far too benign to be an ex-cop.'

Rachel laughed out loud, then said, 'Don't let appearances deceive you, Tom. I assure you, my husband has solved more cases at Scotland Yard than you can shake a stick at.'

'Well that's good to know. Thanks to that feller who bumped off his wife, I'm still marooned on this damn island. First that storm and now the cops tell me to stay put. I can tell you, I can't wait to get away now!'

Suddenly a cabin door flew open and a little girl walked out rubbing her eyes and squinting at the sun. She spoke in a small voice, 'Who are you talking to, Uncle Tom?'

'Ah Samara, my sweet, come here and meet these nice people. They're here from the big house, up yonder on the island.'

As she walked towards them, Rachel thought she had never seen a more enchanting child. The little girl was wearing a simple white cotton shift dress with red rosebuds embroidered on it. She had a beautiful face with delicate features, framed by light brown ringlet curls coming down to her shoulders, grey eyes and freckles on her sunburnt pink cheeks.

'Where's mummy?' she asked plaintively.

Tom replied, 'Mummy'll be back soon, honey. She's just gone to get a few things from the village.'

Jeremy smiled, 'Hello Samara. It's nice to meet you. How do you do?'

Samara replied with a sad look, 'I'm bored. There's nothing to do. I don't like this place. I want to go back to Cairo.'

Tom spoke softly, 'We will, honey, just as soon as these people let us. Meanwhile, let me get these nice new friends of mine, something to drink.' Then turning to Jeremy and Rachel, he asked, 'What's your poison, folks?'

Jeremy replied, 'That's very kind of you. A gin and tonic would hit the spot for both of us, I think.'

As Tom went in to the cabin to get their drinks, Rachel asked the little girl, 'But it's so beautiful here, Samara. Why don't you like it here?'

Samara replied with a serious look on her face, 'Because this place makes mummy unhappy. I want to go to Cairo, where she'll be happy again.'

Rachel asked, 'What makes you think your mummy is unhappy here?'

Samara replied matter-of-factly, 'She's been crying. I don't like to see her cry. People here are mean to her.'

Rachel asked, 'Who's been mean to her?'

'That man who's also from the big house. He was here last night and he made her cry.'

'Really? Can you tell me what he looked like?' Rachel asked tentatively but Samara's attention went to the other side of the boat and she cried out, 'Mummy!'

Bilkis had just returned.

Chapter Nine

Bilkis looked very different. She had no make-up on and looked younger somehow. She was in white palazzos paired with a red halter top. Her hair was tied up in a ponytail. Her face looked pale and serious but as she heard her daughter's voice, her face broke out into a sweet smile. She got down on one knee, as Samara ran to her and put her tiny arms around her neck for a hug. She picked up her daughter in her arms and walked towards Rachel and Jeremy.

She smiled at them, 'Samara tells me you've met her. Where is Tom?'

Jeremy answered, as he got up to pull a chair for her. 'He's in the cabin. He very kindly offered to get us some drinks.'

Rachel said, 'Your daughter is a delightful little girl. She's been giving us company, while Tom is away playing host. Haven't you, Samara?'

Samara gave her a shy smile and turned back to her mother. 'Mummy, what's in the bag? Did you get me a toy?'

'Yes, darling. I got you the wooden boat you liked. Here it is. Now run along and play, ya-habib-albee. Mummy has to talk with these people.'

Samara looked at Rachel and Jeremy and then apparently satisfied that they seemed alright, she left with her toy and went through to the cabins below.

Rachel spoke first, 'We hear that you've been upset.'

Bilkis sighed, 'Yes. It is so sad, no? Anyone would be. It is too upsetting. They've found that poor woman's body with her head bashed in. The news is all over the village. I was with that lady, Madame Zorba when we heard the news.'

Rachel and Jeremy spoke in unison, 'Body? Whose body?'

Bilkis was puzzled. 'Isn't that what you were asking me about, just now? I thought you knew. They found the maid - Dorkas' body, in one of the caves near the Papanos estate's private beach.'

Rachel spoke, 'Dorkas? How awful! But she served us all dinner last night! Are you sure?'

Bilkis nodded, 'Quite sure. The gendarmes went to the Papanos estate to question her about something or the other this morning, and Nerissa - the other maid, told them she was missing since last night. She said the last time she saw her, Dorkas was headed towards the private beach on the estate. Nerissa was upset because the woman did not come back to clean up and Nerissa had to clean up the dinner dishes and tidy up the kitchen all by herself, before retiring for the night. This morning when they searched her room, they found that her bed had not been slept in.'

Rachel gasped, 'Why! We went walking on the same beach last night after dinner and we didn't see her, or anybody else, did we Jeremy?'

Jeremy nodded, 'The crime must have taken place after we retired darling, or we would've seen or heard something. It isn't a very large beach.'

Bilkis said, 'The village gossip mill thinks that someone may have killed her later during the night, or possibly even this morning. Her body was still warm when they found her.'

Rachel shuddered uncharacteristically and wondered what had come over her. She was normally quite matter-of-fact, when it came to dealing with death, in the past. After all, murder cases were part and parcel of her professional life. She wondered if she was going soft.

Jeremy spoke, 'I think we had better head back to the village and find out more.'

Rachel asked, 'What about Stanley's wife, Ariana?'

Bilkis shrugged, 'Still no news about her.'

Rachel spoke, 'Samara mentioned that someone had come up from the main house, to see you last night. Was it Stanley?'

Bilkis looked uncomfortable and shook her head emphatically, 'No! No one came here. Samara told you? She is just a child. She probably dreamt it up. Children can imagine things, you know.'

Rachel said nothing further but wondered why Bilkis was lying. Was she trying to protect herself, or attempting to cover up for whoever she met, the night before.

At that moment, Tom returned with the drinks and food on a tray.

Jeremy got up and spoke, 'I'm afraid we can't stay, old boy. Must head back to the village. Duty calls.'

Tom put the tray on the table and said, 'Oh, duty can wait, old sport. Why don't you just sit back down and have some refreshment? Got you some fresh bread and local goat cheese to munch on.'

Rachel was tempted and the sight of food made her say, 'Oh dear, we did miss breakfast. And it is very kind of you, Tom. I am famished. I'm sure ten minutes won't make a difference either way, Jeremy.'

Jeremy was astonished. He had never known Rachel to give undue importance to a missed meal before, especially when they were in the midst of a case. But he sat back down and said, 'Yes, of course, darling. I am sure it won't.'

He took a sip of his drink, as he questioned Bilkis further about the discovery of the maid's body. From the corner of his eyes, he observed that Rachel was concentrating on eating. He saw her wolf down three large slices of bread with goat cheese. She took a sip of gin and grimaced. She asked Tom, 'I don't want to be a bother, but you wouldn't happen to have some milk on board, would you? I don't know what's come over me but I'd much rather have a glass of milk right now.'

Bilkis smiled as Tom got up. She said, 'Of course, we have milk. A boy comes down to the yacht with fresh goat's milk every morning. The locals are very obliging in these parts.'

Rachel saw the look on Jeremy's face and said, 'I really am very sorry, Miss Hamadi. But I can't seem to control my appetite these days. Must be something in the air here. I feel hungry all the time.'

Jeremy spoke with concern, 'And now that you mention it, you have put on a bit too, darling. I think I ought to take you to see a doctor, once we get back to England. Could be some kind of a thyroid issue.'

Bilkis laughed at them and for the first time, there was a warmth in her smile, as she said, 'You are both detectives, huh? Don't tell me it hasn't occurred to either of you that she could be pregnant? You know Rachel, I was hungry all the time too, when I was pregnant. It is nothing to be ashamed of. Your baby needs the nourishment.'

Rachel's eyes opened wide in astonishment and Jeremy's mouth fell open, as the truth of her words hit home.

Chapter Ten

Jeremy was grinning ear to ear, 'A baby! That explains a lot. I was beginning to worry. You have been looking drawn and tired, darling, not to mention you've been eating an awful lot, you know. Let's sit for a bit.'

'Drawn and tired? And here I thought I was supposed to be glowing in this condition!' Rachel said grumpily.

Jeremy laughed.

They were midway through their walk back from the yacht to the village, having taken the path going up to the hill from the cove. Tall, wild grasses swayed rhythmically to the sea breeze on either side of the mud path. The sun was shining on the turquoise blue sea and they could see sailboats and merchant vessels in the distance. Once they reached the plateau, near the cliff face, Rachel smiled. The view from the cliff was extraordinarily beautiful. She was happy to rest for a while and found a rocky platform nearby, to sit on.

She said, 'Well, we can't be sure yet. I wish you wouldn't get your hopes up, darling. Must get the doctor to confirm but tell me Jeremy, if it does turn out to be a baby, wouldn't it change everything for us? I mean, are we even remotely ready to be parents?'

'If you ask me, I can't speak for myself but I do think you would make a wonderful mother, darling. Besides, it's rather a moot point anyway, isn't it? I don't suppose the baby is going to give us much of a choice now, if he's already on the way!'

Rachel grinned back. 'You seem pretty sure it's going to be a boy.'

'Just a manner of speech. You know, darling, I'd be equally delighted, if not more so, if it turns out to be a little girl. After all, which man in his right mind doesn't fancy the idea of growing old surrounded by beautiful women.'

Suddenly Rachel looked worried, 'Oh dear! It just struck me that Madame Zorba gave me a grave warning about a child. She told me there was danger for a child if I stayed on this island. I didn't put two and two together till now. She told me to go home... oh, Jeremy can't we forget about this case and head home?'

'You're not getting superstitious suddenly, are you? We've been warned off cases on numerous occasions before and you never turned a hair. In fact, I remember when we were at Ravenrock, we got threatening letters and it didn't bother you at all. If anything, it gave you further determination to carry on with the investigation.'

Rachel grimaced, 'Yes, I remember. And I also remember that I got shot at and nearly died! I couldn't bear to put this baby in any danger.'

'And we shan't. As long as you don't scarper off chasing fugitives on your own, like you did at Ravenrock and then in Paris, I can guarantee that you'll be perfectly safe. Besides, I am here to keep you out of harm's way. You have nothing to worry about.'

'You are right, darling. I'm allowing my hormones to turn me into a first-class ninny. Besides, I do want to know what happened here. This is one of the strangest cases we've ever encountered. A disappearance, possibly murder, followed by a sure-shot murder right under our noses. I wonder who is behind it, and what their motive could possibly be!'

'That's my girl! But now I am going to take you back to the Papanos estate and then go off by myself and meet Demakis.'

Rachel said, 'Not on your life, Mister. I'm coming with you!'

As she got up her dress ballooned up again. 'Blast this dress! It's like a blooming parachute!

At least, I'll be safe if someone pushes me off the cliffs around here,' she said with some chagrin.

'Why didn't you wear your trousers, darling? Far more suitable for walks around the island, I should think.'

'As you very kindly mentioned earlier, I've gotten a bit porky. The ones I brought along don't fit me anymore,' she said grumpily.

Jeremy laughed, 'Porky? Never! Pleasantly plump perhaps.'

'Oh, Jeremy, who am I fooling. In the coming months, I'll probably be as big as a house and look ridiculous!'

'I'm sure you'll look lovely, my dear. And you do know that I'll love you just as much even if you become the size of Westminster Abbey. Now, come along. I'll drop you off at the estate.'

'I am not tired, Jeremy. I want to meet Demakis too and find out more about what happened to Dorkas!'

'Steady on, young lady! Let's not get foolhardy. Take some rest. There is no need for you to come traipsing along the countryside with me. And I promise, I shall faithfully report back to you, leaving out no detail whatsoever, about Dorkas' death.'

Rachel sighed, 'Alright, I suppose I could spend some time with Marina and Aristea. For all you know, I may stumble upon something interesting there.

There's something decidedly fishy going on in the Papanos family. There seems to be no love lost among the two women for poor Ariana. Let me see if I can wheedle some information from those two. I might have a dekko around Ariana's room as well, if they'll let me.'

Fifteen minutes later, Rachel was back at the Papanos estate. Jeremy left for the village, after seeing her off at the entrance to the Papanos house. Nerissa let her in and informed her that Aristea was resting in her room and had asked not to be disturbed. Stanley, Stavros and Marina had gone out somewhere, presumably to meet Demakis.

Rachel was left to her own devices. She asked Nerissa to show her the way to Ariana's room. Nerissa shrugged and led the way to the first floor of the beach house and without much ado, opened the second door to the left, along the first-floor hallway. Rachel thanked her and as Nerissa left to get back to her chores, she shut the door behind her. Rachel was finally alone in Ariana's boudoir.

She looked about the stark white-washed room with its wrought-iron bedstead, a sparsely furnished dresser, a large wooden wardrobe and an image of Ariana sprang to her mind. To Rachel's mind, a room could speak volumes about its inhabitants and the clean practicality of this one, somehow took away any romantic notions she had, about Ariana being a wishy-washy sort of woman. Unlike the rest of the house, there were no decorative paintings, knick-knacks and not a single photograph or book to be seen. A potted palm by the window seemed to be the only added decoration. There was a study table and chair near the window. The table's surface held a blotter, a fountain pen in a stand and a bottle of ink and nothing else.

Rachel started by opening the wardrobe. Here too, everything was neatly folded and a few dresses that were hanging, seemed to be of good quality but did not support any designer labels. They were mostly in pastel shades. The drawers had very sensible cotton underclothes, no silk or satin as one would expect a young woman to have but rather the kind that reminded her of granny underwear, designed more for comfort rather than style. If she had not been told that this was Ariana's room, she would have assumed, she had stumbled upon an elderly woman's room. There were three pairs of shoes – a pair of canvas walking shoes and two sturdy pairs of black and brown heels with buckles. There were no sandals, slippers or flip-flops to be seen.

The dressing table was the same. There were just two lipsticks - one light pink and a reddish-brown shade, a jar of cold cream and a box of talcum powder kept on the table. She hoped she would find something in the three drawers below. It was usual for women to keep the surface clean and put messy things like eye-shadow, blushers and mascara in drawers, where they remained out of sight. But as she opened the drawers one by one, she was astonished to find that the drawers were empty! Without even a scrap of paper, a bill, make-up items or anything one would expect to find in a dressing table. They were not even lined with paper or cloth as most drawers usually are.

She looked under the bedclothes and under the pillows. Next, she heaved up the mattress to see if there was anything below it and found nothing. Everything was squeaky clean, which was not odd by itself but the thought went through her mind that even an occupied hotel guest room would have more things in it.

It was simply unnatural. The room was completely incongruous to the image she had of a room that belonged to a shipping magnate's wife, even for someone who rarely hosted parties for her husband, or attended social events. This was more like a nun's room.

And then the thought struck her mind. What if the family had removed everything that Ariana owned, except for the bare necessities before the police could conduct a search? In that case, they would have had to put her things in storage, somewhere on the estate, to be gotten rid of, at a later date. As far as she knew, the house had no attic. She had however noticed that there was an outhouse behind the kitchen garden, which looked like a tool shed or storage area of sorts. She decided to begin her search there.

Chapter Eleven

Meanwhile, at the village lock-up which was fast becoming the nerve centre of police operations, Jeremy found that Dorkas' body had been laid out on ice, in the second room and the local doctor was performing an autopsy behind a shabbily constructed partition, which had been created by using two wooden poles and a ditsy printed floral bedsheet.

Demakis remarked that they now knew the time of death to be between eleven and one, in the early hours of the night before. Her skull had been cracked open by a rock. Now the doctor had to ascertain if she had been hit on the head by a third party, or had fallen and hit her head on the rock.

Demakis explained further, 'The caves are slippery owing to water seepage from above. There are stalagmites and stalactites everywhere. The one she was found in, had dripping water and moss, so it is possible she could have slipped or tripped on a stalagmite, in the dark. We also found a broken lantern next to her. What we need to find out is, what she was doing in the cave, at that godforsaken time of night!'

Jeremy said, 'Perhaps she saw something or someone and decided to follow them or perhaps she was drawn by curiosity to a light in the cave. Have your men searched the cave to see if anyone else had been there? If it was damp, you may be able to get footprints in the muddy areas.'

'We are not, how you British say, complete nincompoops, Mr. Richards. You must give us more credit. Yes, we did find a few interesting things. Two cigarette butts for instance and Dorkas was not a smoker. They were Egyptian - the kind of cigarettes that are sold at the Karalis dry goods store. We also found signs of temporary inhabitation towards the rear of the cave. We found a dry spot with firewood and a blanket. They seemed to be there for a purpose, as though someone had been using that part of the cave for a secret rendezvous. Not only that but there is a tunnel and stone steps leading up to the cellar of a house. It may interest you to know that the house is in fact the Karalis dry goods store!'

'You don't say!'

'The noose tightens around Mr. Karalis' neck.'

'But unless he's a Houdini, I don't see how he could have possibly done this. You had him locked up all night here.' Jeremy said, making a quick motion of his head towards Nikos.

'He may have had accomplices on the outside. We just need to find out who they are.'

Jeremy was not convinced, 'You seem very sure that it was him.'

Demakis shrugged, 'It's either him or the husband. Who else has motive and opportunity?'

'Ah! Now you're asking me to open a can of worms. It could be either of them. But it looks to me, as though you are overlooking the fact, that this crime could also have been committed by a woman. If only we knew how the first...'

Just then a gendarme came in huffing and puffing and interrupted Jeremy in mid-speech. 'Sir, a telegram just arrived from the authorities in Patra. A woman's body has just washed up near the coast with her throat slit and they think it could be Mrs. Papanos!'

Jeremy stood up, 'Good lord!'

Demakis spoke, 'By Zeus! Looks as though you got your wish, eh, Mr. Richards.'

And Jeremy found himself thinking that Demakis was a mind reader. That was indeed what he had been hoping for. A modus operandi for the first murder.

Demakis stood up and walked towards the open doorway through which sunlight was streaming in. He stopped to address Jeremy, 'Come, let's go. There's a Hellenic Gendarmerie speedboat waiting at the cove that should get us to Patra in thirty-five minutes,' then turning to the gendarme, he ordered, 'Get Mr. Stavros or Mr. Stanley, preferably both, down to the cove from the dry goods store. Georgas is taking down their statements there. Tell them they need to come along and identify a body at Patra.'

II

Meanwhile, Rachel was wading through dusty boxes stacked in the dark wooden shed on the Papanos estate. There were broken pieces of furniture and gardening tools on one side. The other side had cardboard boxes and tarpaulin covered boxes. She headed towards them. Sweat was pouring off her head and shoulders. Her dress was feeling itchy in the heat. Sand from the beach had blown in and settled on almost everything. Even the air in that closed space felt gritty.

There was just one skylight in the roof of the wooden shack that had broken glass, possibly from the hurricane that had hit the island a week ago. She looked directly at the floor under it and found no glass pieces. That gave her the added impetus to continue her search. It was obvious that someone had been in here recently and cleaned up the glass. This place wasn't as abandoned as it looked. She almost tripped over a piece of tarpaulin that had been torn off and was caught between two boxes. It was dark in that corner. She wished she had brought a torch along. Removing the tarpaulin, she found a wooden crate. She lifted the lid only to find stacks of old newspapers and magazines. Disappointed, she was about to close the lid and move away from the crate, when her foot accidentally kicked it and a tinkling sound came from somewhere within the crate.

Working quickly, she started lifting the newspaper bundles tied with string. She removed the magazine stacks below that, till she saw a thick cream embroidered cloth with cream tassels on the ends. It looked like a bundle tied with a tablecloth or a bedspread. She untied the knot on the side and smiled to herself as she opened it. She had struck gold.

There were stacks of ladies' clothes, shoes, photo albums and knick-knacks. A glinting object caught her eye. It looked like a thin and flat red Chinese puzzle box, inlaid with a metallic dragon. She had seen something similar in a royal palace in India, where she had solved a historic murder case, which later came to be known as the Riverton Case. She remembered that she had been shown the trick mechanism to open it. She applied pressure on the dragon's head whilst simultaneously pushing on the gilded edge on the opposite side. She heard a click as a slim drawer slid open. Even in the dark, she could see that it contained a few folded papers, perhaps a letter. As she removed the papers, she heard the sound of approaching footsteps.

Thinking fast, she quickly shut the Chinese puzzle box and secreted the folded pieces of paper within the bodice of her dress. She then put the empty box back in the crate and closed the lid. She would have liked to put the newspaper stacks back in, but there wasn't enough time. A part of her wanted to stand there and confront whoever it was with what she had just found. Particularly if it was one of the Papanos family members, but then she remembered that she had promised herself that she'd stay out of harm's way, for her baby's sake. If there was a murderer loose on the estate, she didn't want to confront the person in this shack, without Jeremy by her side. She barely had time to hide behind one of the larger crates before the door creaked open.

It seemed like an interminable amount of time that she stayed crouched in that position. The footsteps seemed to come in her direction. She stiffened. She was glad that she was in a dark corner. She held her breath as the footsteps came closer, then stopped and finally moved away. She couldn't risk peeking out from behind the crate, to see who it was. After a few minutes, she heard the person walk out and shut the door to the shack. She then heard the same footsteps on the path leaving the shack. She felt a deep sense of relief. As she got up from her crouched position, she realised that her heart was beating fast and that she was covered in perspiration.

She waited in silence for ten minutes to make sure that the visitor had left. Then she made her way out of the shack cautiously. She took in huge gulps of fresh sea air, as she walked down the bougainvillaea avenue to the guest cottage. She couldn't wait to get back to her room and see if the paper held any clues, to the crimes being committed on this island. She thought to herself that she would run a cool bath, and then go through her find in peace. Once Jeremy was back she would share what she had found and together they could go back to the shack, and go through the bundle of belongings. She looked forward to confronting the Papanos family about hiding Ariana's belongings, if they were indeed Ariana's. Suddenly it occurred to her that those things could have belonged to the late Delphine as well. The paper secreted within the puzzle box would clarify that.

She was lost in her thoughts when a sudden scuffling movement on the path behind her startled her. Before she could turn around, she felt a blow to the back of her head and then her world went black.

As Rachel lay there unconscious and bleeding, oblivious to the world, her attacker left her lying there and coolly walked off.

Chapter Twelve

Jeremy had returned from the village lockup to the Papanos estate to enquire if Rachel wanted to accompany them to Patra but she was not at the main house. Nerissa informed him that she had stepped out a few minutes ago. He assumed that she had gone back to the guest house, to rest for a while. He decided against disturbing her. He knew that she would jump at the chance of going to Patra when he would have preferred that she take rest.

Five minutes later, Marina came in to the house. She was dressed in a bathrobe and her hair was wet. She had evidently been out for a swim. Jeremy gave her the news about the body found at Patra. He asked if she would like to accompany them to identify the body.

Marina looked shaken, 'It's all too ghastly. I couldn't stand it! You all go ahead. I'll stay here.'

She went to make a drink for herself before going up to change. Jeremy noticed that her hands were shaking as she poured a gin and tonic for herself. Stanley was pacing up and down in the living room as Stavros walked in and asked if they were ready to leave.

Jeremy wrote out a quick note for Rachel, informing her that he would be accompanying the Papanos brothers, to identify the body that had washed up at Patra, and that he would be back in a few hours. He handed it over to Nerissa, who said she would deliver it to the guest cottage.

Half an hour later, they watched from the speedboat as the coastline of Patra approached. Patras, called Patra by the local Greeks was a beautiful ancient town built at the foothills of Mount Panachaikon, on a stretch of land overlooking the Gulf of Patras.

Demakis shouted above the roar of the speedboat, 'We will head to the Achaia City Police headquarters. The body is at the City Police Morgue in the basement.'

Stanley nodded in a dazed fashion and Stavros looked away.

Jeremy hollered, as the spray of the speedboat fanned behind him, 'Would it be possible to ask the medical examiner to come back to Tinios and give us his opinion on Dorkas' autopsy?'

'You mean "her", Demakis shouted back. 'The City Police medical examiner is a woman – Agnieszka Christos. She is also the surgeon at the local hospital in Patra.'

'Right! Would be interesting to see what she makes of this case from a medical standpoint.'

'We shall see! There will be some paperwork involved as the City Police are a sister concern of the Hellenic Gendarmerie. I am hoping they will cooperate,' Demakis replied, as the speedboat cut off the engine and docked.

Ten minutes later they were shown in to the office of the Chief of City Police at Achaia.

The Chief was in his early fifties. He had a military bearing and a greying moustache. He was in plainclothes and wore a navy-blue suit with a deep purple tie. Lieutenant Demakis went in and spoke in Greek for a few minutes and then beckoning Jeremy and the others, he made introductions in English.

The Chief of City Police nodded at them. 'Terrible business, this. I offer my condolences to the Papanos family. Such a tragedy. Lieutenant, we have been in touch with the Hellenic Gendarmerie and they told us where to reach you. I hope you will solve this case and I wish to extend any help that you require. My deputy will see to it,' the Chief said, motioning towards an officer who entered behind them.

As they followed the deputy, he led them down the cool, stone corridors and took the steps that went two levels below the ground floor.

They were shown into the morgue. As soon as the door was closed behind them, Stanley gasped and Jeremy's instant reaction was to pull out his handkerchief and place it on his nose. The smell of putrefying human flesh was overpowering. The body was placed on ice and covered partially in a plastic sheet. There were two people dressed in surgical masks and aprons. One of them looked up and said something sharp in Greek. The other one approached the Deputy with surgical masks.

The Deputy handed them around and said, 'Dr. Christos says you will need these.'

Stanley covered his nose with the mask and approached the table tentatively and then shook his head and shouted, 'No! No! This is not my wife! You have made a mistake. This cannot be her!' he took a few steps back and hurried out of the room.

Stavros was steadier as he approached but upon seeing the bloated discoloured face and hollow fish-eaten eyes, he too stepped backwards in horror. He turned to Demakis, 'There is no way we can identify that. It does not even look human.'

Dr. Christos turned to him and said matter-of-factly, 'A week or so of decomposing in the sea has not been known to improve human appearance! The bloating is also classic and the greenish black skin can give us a pretty accurate picture of the timeline. I would say, she's been in the water for about ten days now. Bloating occurs within three to four days but bodies stay more or less preserved up to seven days in sea water, then decomposition sets in rapidly, especially in warmer waters. Scavengers start attacking and by the second week, the body becomes unrecognizable. Sea-lice, small fish and crab usually eat the softer parts - eyes and the lips. But we can still refer to dental records.'

Stavros stuttered, still in shock, 'I...I don't know if she had any.'

Jeremy spoke kindly, 'Perhaps they could make an identification from personal possessions found with the body. The question is, were there any? Earrings perhaps?'

Dr. Christos spoke in a clipped voice, 'No, the earlobes have been eaten but I did cut a bracelet from the right wrist. It has been handed over to the Evidence Room. I have sent for it. Besides, I have measured the carcass. Stature of about five feet and five inches, light brown hair, colour of eyes unknown. I'd say she was in her late twenties. A cracked skull and a slit throat, which may have been the cause of death, or may have been inflicted by debris or rocks in the sea, post death. Soft tissues and internal organs – stomach, spleen and intestines have dissolved.

Lungs have completely decomposed hence I cannot tell you conclusively if death was caused due to drowning or blunt trauma. Though my personal suspicions veer towards the latter.'

Jeremy asked, 'What about the cervical and thoracic vertebrae?'

Dr. Christos looked up at him sharply. 'I was going to mention it. C7 and T1 are dislodged. Are you a doctor?'

Jeremy shook his head, 'Afraid not. But I used to work for Scotland Yard and I have a fair idea of what to look for in such cases. C7 and T1. That is very interesting.'

Stavros asked Jeremy, 'What does that mean?'

Jeremy answered, 'That means that we cannot overlook death by strangulation.'

Dr. Christos spoke, 'I will not put it in the report, since I do not want to put my professional reputation at stake but if you want my personal opinion, I think someone slit this young woman's throat before throwing her into the sea.'

Just then a gendarme came in, followed by Stanley. He was carrying a small plastic package and handed it over to Demakis. Demakis gingerly took out a silver charm bracelet with small clear crystals embedded in it. He put the packet away and showed them the bracelet.

Stanley nodded and spoke in a broken voice, 'That is my wife's. I could recognise it anywhere. I gifted it to her just before our wedding. The charms are unique. I selected them myself - they symbolise sacred geometry.'

Dr. Christos looked up and spoke, 'I've seen them at souvenir shops in Athens. Are you sure it's hers? I should think these silver and crystal bracelets were common enough in Greece.'

'No. If you look closely you will see that apart from the basic platonic solids, it also has the most sacred of all shapes - a dodecahedron which Plato kept a secret, since it represented a powerful esoteric bridge, a state of marriage between heaven and earth.'

Dr. Christos took a closer look and nodded, 'Yes, that is very interesting. I didn't notice that before.'

'Besides, the bracelet is custom made in platinum and the embedded charms are finely cut diamonds. I doubt you will find something like that in souvenir shops.'

Dr. Christos spoke, 'No wonder it survived. I was wondering how the crystals weren't wrenched away or smashed in the sea, going purely by the condition this body was found in. So, I can take it that this is a positive identification, then?'

Just then the Deputy came back in. 'We have had a telephone call with some bad news from Tinios. Mr. Richards, it seems your wife has been attacked...'

Jeremy gasped, 'Is she alright. Is she...?'

The deputy spoke, 'We think her condition is serious but she is still alive. Mrs. Papanos called and informed us that the local doctor and midwife are taking care of her. They say she has lost a lot of blood. She was found unconscious by Nerissa - the maid on the Papanos Estate.'

Stavros shook his head, 'This is madness. Who could have done such a thing? We will return at once.'

Jeremy turned to the doctor and beseeched her, 'Dr. Christos, please come with us. I fear my wife may be haemorrhaging from a miscarriage. You see, we just recently came to understand that she was pregnant. Please help us.'

Dr. Christos nodded, 'Do you know what her blood type is? I will take some bottles from our blood bank for transfusion.'

As Jeremy answered, Dr. Christos shot into action.

Chapter Thirteen

Rachel was moving in and out of consciousness. At one point, she felt distinctly odd as she hovered over her own body, looking down at the scene below, as though she were watching a movie. She could see a woman in a white coat operating on her. A few more people were in the room. She saw that Jeremy was sitting close by with his head in his hands. Then there was a blinding flash of white light. It felt strangely like the source of all benevolence, golden and warm yet brightly white, and she floated towards it. A memory that this light was no stranger, assured her that she had been with it before. As though, it was the way home somehow. Not the home in the world of man but the true home of her origin.

As she swam in it, in this golden almost fluid radiance, she sensed a joyous freedom beyond all restriction, a limitless vastness enveloped this being of light and she was astonished to find that she was in fact this light, vibrating in oneness with it, swimming in all directions with overwhelming joy and the thinker in her realised the truth. There were many beings swimming in it too in all directions simultaneously. But they were not apart from her! They were individual and different from her but they were her too. For there was no difference between her, those other beings and the fluid light they all moved in. She experienced utter and complete freedom, yet with an incredibly powerful, loving vibrational harmony that no distinctions remained or were even possible and yet every possibility existed. It was she and she was that.

And she was joy, a bliss she had known before, swum in before and this light was love and utter inexplicable bubbling joy. It was new to her, this ever-renewing joy and yet she was aware that she had experienced it before in the recesses of this vast conscious field of her memory. And a great understanding took place. Fear was missing. There was nothing to be afraid of. It was so completely missing that even in the state of light, the very thought that fear was missing astonished her. Everything else besides this joyous truth of bliss and love was a distortion. Truth was that nothing else could pervade the light and limitlessness of consciousness, of this being, her being. 'So, this is my reality', the thinker thought, all the while moving, vibrating and joyously singing with a sound of love that emanated from every part of the oneness.

She swam in this timelessness in all directions. Then the thinker did a strange thing and a thought moved in to the consciousness. Where is Rachel? Where is the body? And she stopped to look at her form and was astonished to find no form at all, just a speck of brightness. Then her physical form slowly reappeared, as she had been on earth and she found herself growing in size and volume from the speck of brightness that she had been. All the other specks swimming around her in the light seemed to shrink, becoming infinitesimally small. In that instant two benevolent beings materialised before her and their light was blinding, so she could not see their faces properly. With infinite compassion they spoke telepathically, 'What are you doing here? You are not supposed to be here. Go back.' And with a flick of movement one of the beings closed the eyelid of the eye which was inexplicably placed across her entire forehead. The eyelid moved from the right side of her forehead and shut on the left side. There was darkness again.

Her consciousness realised that it was back in its form on earth. The sudden separation from the light and the bliss was incredibly painful. She tried in vain to open the eye of consciousness again but instead all she managed to do, was to open her own two limited eyes. The vision was blurred but she could see Jeremy's face above hers.

Jeremy was in tears, 'Oh, thank God, darling. I thought I had lost you.'

She smiled and said clearly, 'Jeremy. I think I've been with God and I saw two of his angels. Do you know my love, that you and I are just thoughts floating in God's mind. We all are.'

Jeremy thought he heard wrong and asked, 'What was that, darling?' but Rachel smiled, as she closed her eyes again.

Dr. Christos moved to examine her patient. She observed, 'She is asleep now.'

Jeremy spoke quietly, 'How can I thank you, Dr. Christos?'

She shook her head in bewilderment and said, 'I'm afraid. I can take no credit. I...I don't know what just happened here. I performed the D & C successfully but she had lost too much blood even before we started the transfusion. Towards the end, she was clinically dead. Her heart had stopped for over ten minutes. I am sure of it. And I have no equipment on this island to revive it. According to medical science she should be brain dead by now and yet she spoke clearly just now.' She moved to take Rachel's pulse and spoke again, 'And now the heart is beating normally.' She shone a small torch under the eyelids. 'And the eye reflex is normal. It is quite unbelievable. She is sleeping normally.'

Marina got up from the armchair in the far corner of the room and said, 'This is a miracle. I think

I shall inform the others.' She left the room, silently closing the door behind her.

Jeremy winced, 'But the baby is gone. I shudder to break the news to her.'

'She is lucky to be alive, Mr. Richards. She is young. And I am sure she will conceive again, should you both wish it. But for now, I will have to say, she must rest for as long as she needs to.'

'Of course, doctor. But I plan to take her back home as soon as possible. When will she be fit to travel?'

'It depends on how fast she recovers from this ordeal. I would not advise any travel for the next week.'

'May I book our passages to England, a week from now, then?'

'Make it ten days, to be on the safe side.'

'Can we at least go by seaplane to Athens?'

'Mr. Richards, I understand your concern in wanting to get her away from this island but I am afraid that until she has healed, it would be foolhardy to travel at all. Internal haemorrhage is a dangerous thing and can recur if the body is not allowed sufficient time to recover.'

Jeremy sighed, 'You are right. I am not thinking straight. She had a premonition about this, you know. She had wanted to leave the island. Now, I wish to God, I had listened to her.'

'There really is no point in berating yourself. No one could have foreseen something like this. And as they say, hindsight is always twenty-twenty.'

'No, it wasn't like that. It seems that the local soothsayer – Madame Zorba or whatever her name is, the woman had warned her she was in danger, or something to that effect but we both brushed it off.'

'I would have brushed it off too. Soothsayers, fortune tellers! Doomsday predictions are their trade in stock, if you ask me. I have no patience with such superstitious, pernicious nonsense and yet...'

At that moment, Madame Zorba and Aristea came into the room and Jeremy and Dr. Christos found themselves exchanging glances. Jeremy grimaced inwardly, as the thought ran through his mind, 'speak of the devil.'

Aristea spoke, 'Jeremy, we heard the news. We will take over now. It has been over three hours. You and Dr. Christos must be exhausted. You both should go, freshen up and eat something. Nerissa has prepared a broth. Go! We'll take care of Rachel and call you as soon as she wakes up.'

Dr. Christos spoke, 'Yes, well. She is out of danger and asleep now. If you find her in any discomfort at all, or if she wakes, call us at once.'

Jeremy thanked them and looked back at Rachel, now sleeping peacefully with a smile on her face. He saw a faint glow around her and somehow, he knew that the danger was past. As they left the room, he turned to Dr. Christos, and said, 'You were close enough to hear what Rachel said about seeing God and angels. Do you think she imagined it?'

'I don't know. Is your wife a very religious person?'

'I can't say that she is. Well, we're not regular church goers, if that's what you're asking.'

'Then from my scientific mind, I could assume that it is probably the after-effects of the anaesthetic. But I really don't know. What just happened in there, is quite frankly inexplicable through scientific reasoning. There's no other way to describe it. It has given me much to think about. Perhaps you can ask her once she's awake.'

Chapter Fourteen

Lieutenant Demakis was shouting at the top of his voice, 'What do you mean, you had to let him go this morning and he gave you the slip!'

Georgas replied nervously, shifting his weight from one leg to another, 'Well, Sir, there are no facilities in this lockup for bathing. He had started stinking and was begging us to let him have a bath. It was only human, Sir. And I only allowed him out for half an hour to go for a bath and a change. I accompanied him to his house myself. Unfortunately, he climbed out of the bathroom window in his house, while I was standing guard outside the door. But we will find him. He couldn't have gone far.'

'You idiot, at around the same time that you foolishly let him out, Mr. Richards' wife was brutally attacked on the Papanos estate. She almost died. This man is dangerous. There have already been two murders and now this inhuman attack on a pregnant woman. And all because you thought you were being human. You imbecile!'

'I am sorry, Sir.'

'I have half a mind to strike you off the force. You are evidently not cut out for this job. You'd be better off selling flowers in Athens.'

'Please Sir, give me a chance. I will find him and drag him back to the lockup myself, Sir.'

'You had better. Now, I have the unpleasant task of facing the Papanos family, to warn them that we have let our prisoner escape. He could be anywhere on this island. You are sure that no fishing boats are missing?'

'Well Sir, there are eight fishing boats that are out in the waters right now. They are all accounted for, but we will know how many return, only by this evening.'

'By Zeus! If even one goes missing, I am going to have your head on a platter for dinner. Meanwhile I shall wire Athens to set up alerts for Nikos Karalis on all ports; and request for more back-up, since the team I have here is absolutely bloody useless. But even before they get here, I want you to get every able-bodied man here, and search every square foot of this place and if he is still on this island, you had better find the fugitive. You must. By God, you've made us look like a pack of fools.'

'Yes, Sir.'

'Proud of it, are we?'

'No, Sir. Sorry, Sir.'

'Get out of my sight!'

Fifteen minutes later, Lieutenant Demakis was at the Papanos estate, relating what had occurred at the lockup earlier in the day. 'I can't begin to express how sorry I am, Mr. Richards. But I assure you we will find him.'

Stavros intervened, 'This time, I suggest you lock Karalis up and throw away the key, Lieutenant!'

Jeremy nodded grimly, 'What else can we do to help you find him?'

'Nothing for now. The villagers are equally outraged and have formed a search party, so he will be found soon, hopefully. For now, I am relieved to know that your wife is out of danger.'

Dr. Christos spoke with anger, 'Not entirely, lieutenant. It is still touch and go. You should know what I know from the injuries, after treating the victim. You should know that this man hit her brutally from the back and as she fell on her abdomen, it caused internal bleeding and a miscarriage. She is very lucky that her skull is intact after a blow like that. I do hope you realise that this can be considered attempted murder.'

Demakis nodded, 'By the time I'm done with him, rest assured that he will go up before a firing squad, for his crimes, Dr. Christos.'

Marina spoke up at this point, 'If it is him. After all, how can you all be so sure it was him?'

Stavros cut her short, 'Oh don't be so stupid, of course it's him. Who else could it be? The rest of us were in Patra at the time.'

Marina replied, 'There's no need to be rude, Stavros. I am merely being cautious. The last thing anyone would want, is to send an innocent man in front of a firing squad.'

II

A few hours later, Aristea walked up to Jeremy, who was napping on an armchair in the living room and gently woke him up, 'She is awake and asking for you.'

Minutes later, Jeremy was at Rachel's side.

'How are you feeling, my darling?' Jeremy asked her, holding her hand gently in his palm.

Rachel said, 'Still a bit groggy. What happened? I keep floating in and out. I can't understand what happened.'

'You are going to be fine, my love. You were attacked and hurt. Dr. Christos came back with us from Patra and operated on you. She says you're out of danger now.'

'The baby?'

'I'm afraid...' Jeremy choked. Tears formed unbidden in his eyes.

Rachel looked at him bewildered and then as she understood, she started weeping. Jeremy sat on the bed and held her as she wept. He was taken aback to feel tears stream down his own face.

'Oh, Jeremy, I thought I was being so careful. I am so sorry.'

'Hush. It's not your fault, darling. It's mine. I should have listened to you when you said you wanted to go home. I wish to God, I had listened to you then.'

Rachel stifled a sob, 'Oh Jeremy, why did this happen to us?'

'I don't know, my love. All I know is that you are here with me. I thank God you are alive.'

'I just wish...'

'Hush. The only thing that matters now is to get you well again and go home. That is the only thing that matters.'

Jeremy climbed on to the bed, beside her and held her as she wept. She stifled a sob and whispered, 'I had the most extraordinary experience, while I was floating, you know. It wasn't a hallucination, I'm sure of it. Neither did it feel like dreaming. It just felt so real, more so than life here that I simply don't know what to make of it.'

'Yes, I can believe that. When you came to, the first thing you said, was that you had seen God and angels.'

'It wasn't so much as seeing God - a face or form. He didn't have one that I could see. It was more like "feeling" God in every part of my being. As though I was a part of him. As though everything was a part of him. It was so joyful, vibrant and radiant – all that light and love, stretching endlessly in every direction. I have no idea why we've always portrayed him as grim and serious, sometimes holding a thunderbolt. The truth is nothing like that. God is simply oneness, great joy and utter freedom from fear. I know that now. It felt as though all lifeforms here, are just thoughts floating in his mind, which is a vast conscious space. I can't begin to describe it really. Words can't do it justice. And there were these beings who looked human but couldn't possibly be human, they simply materialized in that space in front of me and they sent me back. They sent me back through an eye in my forehead.'

'An eye in your forehead? That's interesting.'

'Yes, it is true. The thing is, when I was floating, I didn't have a body. Well not like this one...more like a little speck really. I was a blissful speck swimming through timelessness. It was only when one of those beings reached out and shut my eyelid that I realised that the eye that I was experiencing all this through, was in fact in my forehead because by then I was attached to this body again. Oh, I can't explain it. I know it sounds fantastic but you do believe me, don't you?'

'I do.' Jeremy said softly.

'I suppose if our baby is floating in that radiance and love now, I don't mind it so much, anymore. But I should have liked to hold him in my arms,' she sobbed again. 'But I know he is safe and filled with joy. There's no fear, only love and freedom there.' Rachel said in a small, broken voice and closed her eyes again.

They held each other in silence as Rachel drifted back to sleep in his arms.

Chapter Fifteen

The next day, Lieutenant Demakis was in the Papanos guest cottage. Dr. Christos was there along with Jeremy. Rachel was sitting up in her bed with the help of pillows. She was still drowsy from the medication but Dr. Christos had to return to Patra, and had given Demakis permission to question Rachel, in her presence.

After he had enquired about her health, he asked her point blank, 'Madame, did you get a glimpse of your assailant?'

Rachel responded, 'No, I'm afraid not. The last thing I remember was a sort of shuffling sound behind me, as I was walking on the path back to the guest cottage and then – pain and darkness. Nothing else.'

'We seem to be dealing with a very clever man. But not to worry, we will get him soon.'

Rachel asked him, 'I don't know if it was a man. Unless you have an idea as to who attacked me. Do you have any suspects yet?'

Jeremy answered, 'Lieutenant Demakis thinks it was Karalis. He escaped from the lockup about the same time. I fear he could be right but we thought we would ask you, once you recovered sufficiently, just in case you had caught a glimpse of your attacker.'

Rachel shook her head. 'I can't help you there. But I do remember going into the shed and then someone came in behind me. I couldn't tell if it was a man or a woman but some instinct told me to hide from that person. Whoever it was, left shortly afterwards. But he or she must have waited outside for me and followed me as I left.'

Demakis asked, 'Why would they do that?'

'Possibly to prevent me from snooping any further or to see if I took anything out of the shed.'

Demakis asked puzzled, 'Which shed would this be, Madame?'

'The one behind the kitchen on this estate. It faces the beach. It's a sort of storage hut. I was trying to find something and I did, cleverly hidden beneath piles of old newspapers and magazines. Oh Lord! The Chinese puzzle box. The papers! I found some folded papers in the secret compartment of the box.

And hid them in my dress. Dr. Christos, did you find papers on my person?'

Dr. Christos said vaguely, 'Yes, I think so. I put all your belongings in a brown paper bag and gave them to your husband.'

Jeremy got up, 'I haven't bothered to look inside the bag. I'll just go and check. I left it in the room next door. If I find any papers, I'll fetch them.'

A few minutes later, Jeremy returned triumphantly and laid out two pieces of paper on the coffee table. 'Eureka! They seem to be letters, or rather hurriedly scribbled notes on a hotel's letterhead – Hotel Aphrodite in Athens. This one is dated two months ago. The handwriting is quite illegible but I'll try my best.' Jeremy started reading aloud.

My dear Mouse,

I read your last letter to me with great amusement. On the face of it, it seems, as though my meek little mouse has turned out to be a large, ungrateful and double crossing rat. As for your threats to expose me...Me of all people! I find them most amusing. Who on earth would believe you especially once I tell them about your true antecedents, along with photographic proof. I have enclosed a sample to remind you, my girl. There's plenty more where that came from. Remember the good old days? I certainly do.

Carter

The second letter is shorter and had no date on it.

I am here. You should know well enough by now that I do not take kindly to threats. Bring the fire pearl to me at our designated meeting place today or by God, you shall answer for the consequences. 3PM sharp.

Don't keep me waiting.

Carter

As Jeremy finished, Rachel asked, 'What do you think it means?'

Jeremy shook his head and mumbled, 'I wonder who this Carter chap is?'

Lieutenant Demakis shrugged as he got up to take a closer look, 'Could it be a pseudonym or a code name for Karalis? After all, Karalis and the deceased Mrs. Papanos have a history together. I'll wire Athens and send a team up to Hotel Aphrodite. I know that place well, since it is notorious. It is raided every second month. The owner is Greek - an influential man and we suspect he runs a drug and prostitution ring from there. We'll try and get as much information, on this Carter fellow, as possible. That is, if he ever stayed here. I should like to know who the letter is addressed to. Who's the "Mouse"? And does this have relevance to this case?'

Rachel responded, 'I believe, this has a great relevance to the case, Lieutenant. Because I found these papers secreted in a Chinese puzzle box, among what I believe to be - Ariana's belongings, which the family secreted away for some reason before your men could search her room.'

'Why would they do that?'

'You would have to ask them that, but I think they all know a lot more about her disappearance than they're letting on. Hence, I am not ruling out the fact that it could have been someone in the Papanos family, who attacked me, to prevent me from finding something they are all desperately trying to hide.'

Jeremy spoke, 'But we all left for Patra about the same time you were attacked, which I reckon was around noon.'

'I am certain I was attacked before that. It was only about eleven 'o'clock when I finished searching Ariana's room and since I could not have spent more than twenty minutes at the shed, I think you all left for Patra after I was attacked.'

'Good Lord!' Jeremy exclaimed.

Dr. Christos said, 'Considering the amount of blood loss, I'd say it was possible.'

Rachel spoke, 'So you see. It might have been anyone. Now, putting myself in Ariana's shoes, if I were blackmailing someone or being blackmailed, I would make sure no one else could find these incriminating letters. And you see, I think Ariana hid it in a Chinese puzzle box with a tricky mechanism, which she alone knew how to operate.'

'Go on.'

'I also think that either Ariana herself was the recipient of the letters or she found this letter and was blackmailing someone else, possibly another woman. The mouse is definitely a woman. I think it quite likely that it could be someone in this household.' Then turning to Jeremy, she asked, 'Was there a photograph with this?'

Jeremy blushed, 'As a matter of fact, I was just about to mention it. A small black and white photograph of a very scantily clad young woman fell out, when I unfolded the papers. Her face is in shadow but the body is completely visible. There's a note scribbled on the back. It says, "Remember 1937."'

Dr. Christos spoke in a professional tone, 'Might I take a look?'

Jeremy took it out of his pocket and handed it over.

Dr. Christos glanced at it and said tonelessly, 'I wouldn't call this scantily clad. She's practically nude. Most definitely a brunette, possibly Greek or middle-eastern, very young as her body is still developing hence not very well proportioned, about sixteen or seventeen years old, and judging by the chair on which she is posing, I'd say about 5' 4" or 5' 5". A pity the head is thrown back and her face is not visible. If this photograph was in fact taken in 1937, and is over ten years old or more, it could be a close match to the body in the morgue but I can't be sure since the body was in an advanced stage of decomposition. Perhaps we ought to ask the husband.' She got up to hand the picture to Rachel.

Rachel looked at it and shook her head, 'Not yet, surely. The date on the picture may just be an additional threat, something that refers to an event that occurred in 1937. The picture itself may have been shot even earlier than 1937. In that case, it could be anyone with a past they would like to conceal. Marina perhaps or even Bilkis Hamadi! We need to find out more about all of them. Especially Ariana - like where she came from, who her parents were, if she has any family back in Athens, presuming she grew up there.'

Demakis responded, 'It cannot be Marina Papanos, as she hails from a very old and well-known family in Greece and must have been very carefully brought up. But it could be Ariana Papanos. From my interrogation of the Papanos family, I gathered that she was orphaned and brought up by an aunt and uncle in Athens. The aunt passed away in 1931. According to Stanley Papanos, she had cut ties with her uncle long ago and had no one else in the world.'

Jeremy spoke, 'How convenient! But if I were you, I'd find this uncle's current whereabouts. He may even have some connection with this Carter character, especially if the girl in the picture is Ariana.

Considering she was just a child of sixteen, when this picture was taken.'

Demakis nodded grimly, 'I shall make this my priority and head back to Athens today, and find out what I can about this Carter person and what connection he has with the Hotel Aphrodite, if any. If we are lucky, he may still be a guest there and we'll nab him.' With that Demakis got up and left the guest cottage.

A few minutes after he left, as Dr. Christos was dosing Rachel with barbiturates, Rachel exclaimed, 'Oh shoot! I forgot to remind Lieutenant Demakis to ask the Papanos family about the fire pearl.'

Jeremy's eye brow went up. 'Ah yes, I wanted to ask you about it. What on earth is a fire pearl? And what do you know about it?'

Rachel replied, stifling a yawn as the strong dose of barbiturates began to hit her, 'All I know is that it's a Javanese gem, a meteorite or tektite of some sort called the fire pearl. I think we need to ascertain if it has been stolen from the household, or if it is still here in Aristea's collection. I was given to believe that it is a very valuable gem and highly prized by the Papanos family as a lucky charm.'

Jeremy looked bewildered, 'This case gets stranger and stranger by the minute. But you deserve a rest now. Leave it to me, darling.'

Chapter Sixteen

Georgas came in through the gate of the Papanos estate just as Lieutenant Demakis was leaving and announced triumphantly, 'Sir, we've found him! We've caught Nikos Karalis! While I was searching the caves with the search party, a few villagers found him hiding in a goat shed near the cove. It seems that the boy Dimitri – the goatherd had helped him hide but his mother noticed that Dimitri was smuggling bread into the goat shed and when she questioned him, the boy got scared and ran away. She raised an alarm and the villagers finding the shed locked, broke down the door. They found him cowering inside and dragged him back to the lockup.'

Demakis nodded, 'Some war hero! I want him taken to the cells in Athens today.'

Georgas responded cheerfully, 'Yes, Sir. I will do the needful, Sir.'

Demakis looked to the horizon and said, 'On second thoughts, I think I will accompany the prisoner myself. I am not taking any further chances.'

Glancing back at Georgas' crestfallen face, Demakis added, 'It's not that I don't trust you. I do have to carry out further investigations in Athens, which I will attend to, after seeing that our prisoner is safely locked away.'

'Yes, Sir!'

'I want you to stay here and keep an eye on things at the Papanos Estate. Some information has recently come my way that the attack on Madame Rachel may have been committed by someone else.'

'I was about to say, Sir, that Karalis could not have attacked Madame Rachel after his escape, as at the time of the attack, he was on the other side of the island. The boy - Dimitri's story also confirms it. Perhaps that lets him off, Sir.'

'That does not let him off, Georgas! Not by a long shot. There are two other murders he has been linked to; Ariana Papanos' wedding ring was found along with his bloodstained shirt at his store and don't forget that the maid - Dorkas' body was found in the cave leading up to his cellar. That reminds me, I want the shed behind the kitchen on this estate searched again.'

Georgas looked puzzled, 'We searched there already, Sir. It was full of junk.'

'You missed vital evidence. There is a crate there with a bundle containing the late Ariana Papanos' belongings. Madame Rachel said that she found her things cleverly hidden under piles of old newspapers and magazines.'

'Oh, I see! I'll get to it immediately, Sir.'

'Once you get the bundle, I want you to take it to the lockup where you can go through it with a fine-tooth comb. And then, I want you to partner Mr. Richards in your official capacity. Hand over this letter to him. I am giving him the authority to question the Papanos family members regarding the murdered woman's belongings being stashed away. In the letter, I have also requested him to question the family members regarding their whereabouts, at the time his wife was attacked and I want you to be present there and take everyone's statements.'

Georgas looked unsure, 'But Sir, wouldn't it be better if you were to question the family?'

Demakis replied, 'No, I cannot. There is something of vital importance that I need to do now. I have to follow up an important lead to Hotel Aphrodite in Athens which may break this case wide open.'

'Ah! I see, Sir.'

'And Georgas, after you are done taking statements at the Papanos house, I want you to continue to question people around in the village. Someone must know something. We have to get to the bottom of the maid Dorkas' murder as well. The two are definitely linked.'

'Yes, Sir!'

II

Back at the Papanos estate, the family was gathered in the study. Jeremy had just asked to see the fire pearl and Aristea had gotten up to retrieve it from the cabinet behind her armchair. Aristea turned around, her face ashen, 'It's missing! The fire pearl is gone from the crystal cabinet! I don't understand it! It is not possible.'

Stavros jumped up from his chair in the study, 'What do you mean it's gone, Grandmamma? You said you got it back! Kept it safe, I mean.'

'I did! It was there in the cabinet just a week ago. Stanley put it in there himself. I saw it. Marina saw it! And look, the lock has been tampered with. Someone has stolen it only recently. These scratches on the wood were not there a few days ago!'

Jeremy asked, 'Are you sure?' He moved forward and bent down to examine the lock.

Stanley interjected, 'Well, it's small. It may have rolled off somewhere. Look again in the glass cabinet.'

Aristea lost her temper, 'Why don't you take a look? As far as I know, it has never rolled off in all these years and I don't see why it should now!'

Jeremy shook his head from his crouched position in front of the cabinet, 'I daresay you've been robbed. I can tell that this lock has been broken. And Aristea is right, the scratches on the veneer are fairly recent.'

Marina blurted out, 'But Ariana is dead. Who else could have…?'

Jeremy got up and gave her a meaningful stare and then looked at all of them one by one. He finally spoke, 'Look here. Why don't you all sit down and make a clean breast of things. Rachel is absolutely convinced that you all know what happened to Ariana and your inferences lead me to believe that she is right.'

Stanley stuttered, 'I…I don't know what you're talking about.'

Jeremy responded, 'I should think that it wouldn't take more than average intelligence, to understand my import, Stanley. Stavros just let it slip that you got the fire pearl back. From whom, I'd like to know? And Marina, what do you know about it? Did you catch Ariana trying to steal it? What actually happened the day she went missing?'

There was pin drop silence.

Aristea finally sighed and said, 'If we tell you what really happened, you wouldn't believe us.'

Stanley shouted, 'Grandmamma, No!'

Jeremy lifted a hand towards Stanley to silence him and responded quietly to Aristea, 'Try me.'

Aristea started speaking, 'To truly understand what happened here that night, I have to take you back in time when Kosta – my son, was still alive. When he was a young man of twenty, he started a business. He had one ship that he had salvaged from the scrap yard and he spent all our family's savings to fix it up and make it seaworthy again. It was then used to transport cargo to the east – Sumatra, Java and Malaya. For three years, he travelled with the ship and while he did not earn much, since most of the profits from the venture went towards the upkeep and repair of the junk, he seemed happy enough. We were still poor. We had enough to eat and a roof over our heads, so I had no complaints. He continued to travel. From one such trip he came back elated. He told me he had acquired a very rare and mystical object called a fire pearl. He informed me that this was going to make him rich beyond his wildest dreams.'

She paused to pour water from a carafe into a glass and take a sip, 'I of course was happy for him but put aside his outrageous claims of the fire pearl's mythical powers. I naturally put it down to the fanciful superstitions of the East and took no further notice. But soon after he got back from that trip, within a week, things started happening. First, he got an offer to buy another ship for next to nothing, and then three months later another and so on, until he had enough money to start buying new ships. Business deals seemed to materialize out of thin air. Contracts that had belonged to much larger and well established shipping firms began to fall into his lap. Important people began to take notice of him. Before long he was on a success trajectory that far outrivalled his competitors. And he credited it all to the fire pearl. And had I not witnessed his meteoric rise, since the object came into his possession, I would not have believed it myself, Mr. Richards. But there it was. Within five years of acquiring the fire pearl, he became one of the richest men in Greece.

Then he met and married Delphine and they had their first child. We were a happy family. But no life is always consistently happy. The Gods like to play their games. When Delphine was carrying Stanley, Kosta's friend – Spiros, came here to stay with his wife, Zaida. She was a pleasant, homely woman. Not very bright but men don't really need intelligence in their women, do they? She was a peasant in terms of education but she had a beautiful accommodating nature. Far too accommodating. Within a month of their arrival, she was making large meals and Kosta was constantly going to spend time with them, in the evenings. Delphine had left a month before that for England, to deliver her baby in her mother's home in Sussex. Kosta travelled a lot between Athens and Tinios. He had even sent Spiros to Athens, to temporarily help with some work in his office there. I suppose Kosta was lonely whenever he was home on this island. Hence, Kosta and Zaida spent a lot of time together without either of their spouses. Nine months later, Zaida delivered a baby boy – Nikos.'

Jeremy asked, 'Am I to infer from all this that Nikos is your illegitimate grandson?'

Aristea shrugged, 'Infer what you will. But know this - my Kosta saw to the boy's education and took an interest in that boy that goes beyond the ordinary.'

Stavros shook his head, 'I don't believe it for one moment. Our father was simply a generous man, who helped a friend cum employee's son. If you ask me, I think grandmamma has a fanciful and vivid imagination.'

Stanley interjected, 'And if that had been the case, our father would have left some provision for him in his will, which he clearly did not. That village bumpkin is definitely not our half-brother.'

Aristea raised an eyebrow, 'Yet you saw it fit to steal his girlfriend from under his nose.'

Stanley retorted, 'She chose me, Grandmamma! Anyhow, I regret I ever set eyes on her now.'

Jeremy interjected, 'That's all very well but I'd appreciate it if you could tell me how it is linked to Ariana's recent disappearance and death? Are you suggesting that Nikos is behind it all, out of some sense of vengeance?'

Aristea sighed and said, 'I am coming to that, if you'll only have a bit of patience with the meandering reminiscences of an old lady.'

'I am sorry. I shan't interrupt again. Please continue.'

But before she could continue, Nerissa poked her head through the door and announced, 'A gendarme is here for Mr. Richards. He says he has a message from Lieutenant Demakis.'

Jeremy spoke irritably, 'Oh dash it all! I wonder what it is now! Mrs. Papanos, and the rest of you, please don't go away. I am very keen to continue our conversation. But I'm afraid, I must attend to police business. I shall be back soon.' With that he left the room.

Chapter Seventeen

Georgas was waiting for Jeremy in the hall.

'What is this message you've brought?' Jeremy enquired.

Georgas handed him the letter Demakis had left for him. As Jeremy read it, Georgas said, 'Well Sir, Lieutenant Demakis wanted me to take statements regarding everybody's whereabouts, at the time your wife was attacked. And he believes that someone in the family is responsible for hiding Mrs. Ariana Papanos' belongings in the shed. I have retrieved them and placed them in the lockup. I am to take notes while you question them about that as well.'

'Well, this is rather unorthodox, even by Greek standards. I can hardly hold an official interrogation here. These people are my hosts. Where is your

Lieutenant Demakis anyway? Why can't he do it himself?'

'He's half way to Athens by now, Sir. He is shifting the prisoner - Karalis to the lockup at the Hellenic Gendarmerie Headquarters today. And he mentioned that he has some important business to attend to, something about investigating a certain hotel in Athens as well.'

'Well, well, he certainly doesn't let moss grow under his feet, does he?'

Georgas was perplexed, 'I am not aware that he suffers from any foot infections, Sir.'

'Never mind, Georgas. It was just a figure of speech. As it stands, you are in luck. The family is gathered in the study. But before we start, I would like you to give me a little time. I was in the middle of something and I need to tie up some loose ends. Meanwhile, why don't you go to the kitchen and get a bite to eat. I'm sure Nerissa will be obliging. I'll call you once I am ready.'

Georgas replied with uncertainty in his voice, 'I think I'll just wait here, Sir.'

'Alright, suit yourself. Take a seat. Read a newspaper. I'll call you in a bit.'

Georgas nodded nervously, as Jeremy walked back to the study. He could hear raised voices within the room. He heard Stavros say, 'Grandmamma, you mustn't tell him about this, you can't. I know Jeremy

Richards better than all of you. He may be my friend but first and foremost, he is a man of principles. And if you tell him what Stanley, you and Marina did, he will not hesitate to hand you all over to Demakis. Is that what you want, Grandmamma? To spend your golden years in a sordid jail cell!'

Marina wailed, 'Oh, Grandmamma, you can't do this to me. I was only thinking of protecting the family. I don't see why I should suffer for what any decent upstanding person would have done, in my shoes.'

Stavros spoke again, 'For once, I agree with my wife. I see no point in it.'

Aristea said with anger, 'That girl is dead, Marina. Dead! I never thought she would die! And if you have any conscience at all, which I am very much beginning to doubt, we must tell him our version of events, of what actually happened.'

Stanley started to say, 'But I thought you...'

Aristea interrupted him, 'You are not very bright, Stanley, I know what you thought and you got it wrong, as usual.'

Marina was wailing again, 'You are right, she's dead, Grandmamma. Dead! And nothing you do now, can bring her back to life. Why don't you think about those who are still alive? I don't want to spend the rest of my life in jail...'

Aristea said, 'I can still hear Kosta's voice, telling us that if we ever lost the fire pearl, only misfortune would follow and now I believe him.'

Jeremy had heard enough. He opened the door and walked in. Suddenly there was utter silence except for Marina, who was still sniffling into her handkerchief.

He addressed them all, 'I see I've caused quite a storm in a teacup. I'm afraid, I couldn't help eavesdropping a bit. Look, I know what you all think but I honestly think Aristea is right. Whatever happened, it will be better to come clean. I speak from my years of experience with Scotland Yard. If Ariana's death was accidental, and you had anything to do with it, you can still get the best legal help that money can buy. I am sure you can come out of it with proper representation. Concealing the facts will not help. The truth will out, eventually, and you should know that.'

Stavros said, 'Yes, I agree with you on one point, Jeremy. The fact that you have years of experience with the law in England. But you forget that we are not in England. Here in Greece, the law unequivocally states that a person is considered guilty unless proven innocent. My grandmother is aged and does not understand these things. Why should I allow my family to be persecuted by the law here? I forbid her to say anything more about it. And I hope as my friend, you will understand my stance.'

With that Stavros opened the door and motioned Jeremy to follow him out. As they walked down the corridor Jeremy spoke, 'I do understand. And I hope that you understand that I need to question all your movements for the time that my wife was attacked on your premises. At the moment, there is a gendarme waiting outside to take your statements.'

Stavros was flabbergasted. 'Surely, you don't think that any member of my family had anything to do with the cowardly attack on Rachel?'

Jeremy lost his temper. 'I am sorry, Stavros, but in light of the recent revelations from your family that I could not help but overhear, I don't know what to think anymore. The fact remains that one of your own family members – Ariana, was murdered on this property, not to mention the maid – Dorkas, was killed soon after the event. Perhaps because she could reveal too much about Ariana's murder. And then my wife was attacked, when she found some critical evidence regarding Ariana's death. Three brutal attacks on this property on three helpless women, and now, you have prevented Aristea - the one person who seems to have any sort of conscience here, to speak the truth. I suggest you rethink your position, before you play the injured party.'

Stavros stopped and turned to look Jeremy in the eye, 'If that is your view, my dear Jeremy, I think we shall all be happy to give the gendarme our statements. However, as the head of the Papanos family, I must reiterate that you desist from questioning any member of my family, any further. Might I remind you, that you are not here in any official capacity but in fact a guest in our family home.'

Jeremy responded, 'I need no reminders on that point, my dear Stavros. I do apologise for losing my temper. And yes, I am perfectly aware that I may not be part of the official investigative team here, nor do I wish to be. I am merely acting under orders from your Lieutenant Demakis. I think it only fair to tell you that he will be back from Athens by tomorrow morning and I daresay, you will not be able to avoid further questioning from him.'

Stavros replied, 'Thank you, Jeremy. We shall prepare ourselves. Now if you'll excuse me, I need to telephone Athens. Our yacht is scheduled to arrive back here tomorrow, after repairs. I shall request our family lawyer to board it and join us on Tinios, to be a part of any official interrogation from this point forth. You do understand that I wish to get to the bottom of this mess myself but I will not allow my family to be persecuted or treated like criminals. I hope there are no hard feelings between us?'

'None at all, old chap and I do understand. We all want to protect our families. Given that my wife was one of the victims in this case, I will leave no stone unturned, to find out who is behind it all. I hope you realise that I now have equal motivation, to get to the bottom of this, as much as you do.'

Stavros smiled, 'Now come, let's set our differences aside for old times' sake. The yacht should be back here tomorrow in tip-top shape and if Rachel is up to it, perhaps we can all board it the day after. The fresh sea air will do her a world of good.'

Jeremy nodded, 'I think she'll like that. I'm all for it, if Demakis will let us.'

Stavros nodded, 'Certainly. We shall take permission from Lieutenant Demakis. He can even come along, if he likes. To be honest, I've missed the yacht. I just want to test her performance after a month of repairs. We'll just take a small cruise around the island and back.

Chapter Eighteen

A few hours later, just as the sun was about to set, Rachel had unexpected visitors in the guest cottage. There was a discreet knock on her door and as it opened, she saw little Samara holding flowers. Bilkis smiled at her, as she followed her daughter into Rachel's room.

'Oh! How lovely!' Rachel said, as she sat up in bed and accepted the bunch of wildflowers that Samara had brought for her. Samara smiled shyly.

Bilkis spoke with pride in her voice, 'She picked them herself.'

Rachel smiled back, 'And they are beautiful. Thank you! I think I needed flowers. I've been cooped up in here for two days now.'

Bilkis pulled up a wicker chair near Rachel's bedside and sat down. 'We heard what happened and I had to come and see you. I wanted to avoid the family up at the main house, so I came the back way. We sneaked up from the beach.'

'Ah, yes, very clever of you. Jeremy and I have used that path behind the cottage quite a few times, to go to the village.'

Bilkis turned to Samara and said, 'Darling, mummy needs to say something to Rachel in private. Could you go and play outside?' Samara nodded and Bilkis added, 'Play where I can see you, through the windows, okay? Don't go far.'

As Samara skipped out, Bilkis' voice became serious, 'I was devastated to hear that you were so badly hurt. I am so sorry. How are you feeling now?'

Rachel replied, 'I am much better now, thanks. I don't think I even need the barbiturates anymore. If it wasn't for the doctor's insistence that I take at least forty-eight hours' bedrest, I would have been up and about by now.'

'No, you need to rest. I know that you lost the baby. I am really truly sorry. It must have been awful,' Bilkis said, putting her hand over Rachel's.

Rachel was moved by her kindness. 'Yes. I try not to think about it much. I didn't have much time to even get used to the idea that I was pregnant, you see. It all happened so quickly. You suggested that I could be pregnant in the morning and then this happened a few hours later.'

Bilkis asked, 'Oh! When exactly did it happen? Did you see who...'

'No. I have no idea who hit me. I don't even know if it was a man or a woman. But I know the approximate time. Somewhere between eleven thirty and noon yesterday. That's just my surmise. I wasn't wearing my wrist watch.'

Bilkis looked reflective, 'I see.'

'Why do you ask?' Rachel queried.

'Oh, nothing. I just wondered.'

'What?'

Bilkis spoke, 'Well, Tom said he was walking on the cliffs above at eleven thirty or so and he happened to look down towards the beach and saw a middle-aged woman come out of the water and walk towards the path up to the Papanos house. I think it must have been Stavros' wife, Marina. It had to be. Because there is no other middle aged woman on this property.' She made a face.

Rachel's eyes opened wide, 'But then she may have seen the person who attacked me!'

Bilkis raised an eyebrow, 'Or, she may have been the one who attacked you. You just said you didn't know if it was a man or a woman. I wouldn't put it past her. She can be quite vicious. But as much as I despise that woman, even I can't pin a motive on her for attacking you!'

'Oh, but I can! Bilkis, I don't know why I'm telling you this but I do think that someone in the Papanos family is trying to hide something. And I found two notes and a photograph that positively reeks of blackmail. Now this is only temporarily in my care, as it will be handed over to the police as evidence, as soon as Lieutenant Demakis returns but here, let me show you.' Rachel reached out to the drawer beside her bedside and retrieved one of the notes.

Rachel was looking at Bilkis very closely, as she handed her the note.

Bilkis' face went white and her hand shot to her mouth to stifle a gasp. And just as quickly, she regained her composure.

Rachel asked, 'What is it? Do you know this handwriting? Or who this Carter person is?'

Bilkis shook her head, 'No. No. It isn't that. It is the letterhead. It gave me a shock. Do you remember that I told you that I had recently performed in Athens?'

'Yes.'

'Well, my performance was at Hotel Aphrodite. They invite me to perform there every year. I know the owner well. His name is Aleksy Bemus.'

'I see.'

'No, you don't see. Apart from this hotel, Aleksy has many other businesses and while some are rumoured to be a bit shady, he is known to be one of the biggest financiers in Greece. And this might interest you - he happens to be a very close associate of Stavros Papanos. In fact, their association goes back a long way. Received wisdom is that the Papanos empire is where it is today, mainly because of Aleksy Bemus' constant and timely financial aid.'

Rachel was intrigued. 'You don't say! I find that very interesting.'

'And I will ask Tom if he knows anyone by the name of Carter. If this person stayed there in the past two months, Tom will surely have run into him given that he has a permanent suite of rooms booked for his use at the Aphrodite. He knows almost everyone there.'

Rachel nodded, 'Oh, yes, if Mr. Preston can throw some light on our unknown blackmailer that will help us enormously.'

Bilkis said, 'I will ask him. Now I must go. It will get dark soon. Samara cannot walk very fast and the cliff path is not very well lit.'

Rachel nodded and said, 'Tread carefully and say goodbye to Samara for me.'

As Bilkis got up to leave, Jeremy entered the room and said, 'I thought I'd see you here. I just met Samara playing outside.'

Bilkis smiled at him and said, 'I was just leaving. But I'll be back tomorrow. Your wife has given me a job to do.' With that she winked at Rachel and sashayed out of the room.

Chapter Nineteen

Jeremy raised an eyebrow, 'What was that all about?'

Rachel smiled at him, 'I'll tell you all about it. How are things up at the house?'

'Not very good, I'm afraid. You were right all along. The entire family is involved in some way. And Aristea was almost about to confess what she knew about it, when that bumbling jackanapes -gendarme Georgas interrupted us. Then by the time I got back to the room, Stavros got all uptight and prevented Aristea from spilling the beans. He's scared to death about something. They all are.'

'What about the fire pearl?'

Jeremy answered, 'It's stolen alright and Aristea gave me some long-winded story, about how they are all convinced that the fire pearl was responsible for the success of the Papanos empire, and they are equally convinced that there's only doom and gloom in store for them now that it's been filched. The import I got from that entire talk was that someone, possibly Ariana, attempted to steal it sometime ago, but they managed to get it back. And I am almost tempted to believe that Ariana was accidentally bumped off in the process. They're all barmy - the lot of them! And now it's been stolen again, by yet another party. I am at my wit's end. I find it very hard to believe that this whole case revolves around a silly little rock, a meteorite of all things.'

'Perhaps it really is special. People have killed for diamonds and rubies, why not a fire pearl that is supposed to bestow untold wealth and success on its owner?'

'Not you too! But let's say, you are right. Apart from the Papanos family, who else would value the fire pearl so highly and covet it so badly that they would be willing to kill for it? Do you suppose Bilkis and that playboy of hers could be involved?'

Rachel answered, 'I don't think Bilkis is. She just finished telling me that the owner of Hotel Aphrodite – a certain Mr. Bemus, who happens to be a bigwig financier in these parts, is credited with the success of the Papanos shipping empire.'

'What about Tom Preston? He's a geologist. They collect rocks and things, don't they?' Jeremy asked.

Rachel shook her head, 'They probably do but I very much doubt that the playboy would stick his neck out and go around killing people for it. And why would he need the fire pearl, in the first place? He's rich enough as it is and will probably inherit millions more once his old uncle pops it.'

Jeremy thought out loud, 'Yes you are right. It doesn't make any sense.'

Rachel mused, 'Our blackmailer, Carter certainly showed a great interest in it.'

Jeremy said, 'Yes, but he isn't on the island, is he?'

'Perhaps he was and when Ariana didn't show up with the fire pearl, he just legged it out of here. No, that sounds lame, even to me,' Rachel grimaced as Jeremy grinned at her.

Jeremy spoke, 'It all keeps coming back to Nikos Karalis. Do you know, Aristea thinks that Nikos is in fact her illegitimate grandson?'

'Are you serious?' Rachel asked wide eyed.

'Yes, that was an elaborate part of the story she narrated before Stavros put a gag order on her. Apparently, Kosta and Nikos' mother had a thing going long back.'

Rachel said, 'Well, if he grew up here, hearing stories of the magical fire pearl from his mother, he may be just as convinced as they are, about the fire pearl's mythical attributes. Perhaps he managed to convince himself that if he could take it, it could change his fortunes as well. And poor chap, he could use a leg up. If Aristea is to be believed, first he's born illegitimate, cast aside by his real father and brothers. He grows up in a different class from his brothers and then his fiancé throws him over and ends up marrying one of his rich brothers. Rum luck, don't you think?'

'Or maybe it's all hogwash and a very clever ruse, which Aristea used, to cast suspicion on him and away from her own family.'

Rachel rolled her eyes, 'A tall order. I am convinced the family is involved. And by the way, Bilkis told me that Tom was on the cliffs yesterday around noon and spotted a middle-aged woman coming out of the sea after bathing. Bilkis is also convinced that it was Marina and now I suspect that Marina could have spotted me from the sea. She saw me entering the shed and then scared that I would find something incriminating like Ariana's belongings, she followed me there. She realised that I had opened the crate, the one in which they had hidden Ariana's things. Then in a blind panic, not knowing what else to do, she coshed me.'

'My goodness, you could be right. She did come in to the house with her hair all wet, wearing a bathrobe just before we left for Patra. As I recall, her hand was shaking as she poured herself a drink. I did think it odd at the time but I put it down to the news that Ariana's body had just been discovered.'

'That's a reasonable explanation but if it was her, we have no proof. And we'll have the dickens of a time trying to get any evidence to support my theory. The family will probably be falling over each other by now to create alibis for one another.'

Jeremy interjected, 'I agree. But chin up, the cracks are beginning to show and somethings bound to turn up sooner or later. By the way, while we're on the subject of this family, we've been invited by them to go on a short yachting trip around the island, the day after. Apparently, Stavros sent the yacht for repairs a while ago and it will be back at Tinios tomorrow. He said something about testing her speed and performance. But we'll accept the invitation, only if you're up for it. We don't have to go.'

'Oh Jeremy, I'm fine already. Despite being coshed and almost bleeding to death, strangely enough, I feel fit as a fiddle. There is absolutely no pain whatsoever. Even the grief I felt at losing our baby seems to have been miraculously lifted. Every time I think about it, I hear a calming voice in my head, telling me that everything happens for a very good reason, even if the reason isn't apparent now. I have a peculiar idea that the golden light I was floating in, whilst I was unconscious, healed me completely. In fact, I am taking medicines just because I've been told to, but honestly I don't feel ill at all.'

'My God, there must be something about the air on this island. People believing in magical fire pearls, your vision of golden light and spontaneous healing. If I'm not careful, I'll be seeing fairies next.'

'Jeremy!'

'Sorry darling, it's not as though I don't believe you, I honestly do. Even the doctor was puzzled by your recovery. She said it was quite inexplicable from a medical standpoint. I just think that the stress of the past few days is beginning to tell on me. I can't wait for Demakis to get back tomorrow with the good news that he has found and arrested Carter. I just want all this to be over so we can head back home.'

'Even if he does, I'm not sure arresting Carter will give us all the answers. Besides, you do realise that it will be miserably cold in England right now, darling. Probably raining cats and dogs too,' Rachel reminded him.

'You know, I wouldn't mind that one bit, sitting in front of a crackling fire with Toby by our side, as the rain clatters down. I don't know how these adventurous chaps do it – spend years and years away from home without turning a hair. Greece may be a sunny and beautiful paradise, but by God, I'd give anything to be on a boat back to England right now.'

Chapter Twenty

Demakis was back on the island. He paid Jeremy and Rachel a visit at the guest cottage.

He was not a happy man. 'I can't understand it. I went personally to the Hotel Aphrodite to check the guest registers, to see if anybody called Carter had stayed there and nobody by that name has checked in or stayed at the hotel in the recent past. I had my men go through historical registers - up to ten years ago. I also got them to check other hotels in the vicinity.'

Jeremy looked at him, 'I would have done the same. After all, there is always the possibility that he simply used the hotel notepaper without ever having stayed there.'

'We checked with the staff there. The manager, who has run the place for the past forty years told me that the only person he could think of, was a man from New York called Andrew Carter, who died in the hotel fire in 1939. It seems that the entire south wing of the Hotel Aphrodite had been completely gutted. The only reason he remembered the name so well was because thirteen people died that night and Andrew Carter was one of them. The firemen had recovered his body from his room, burnt to a crisp, and the night porter later identified him through the distinctive signet ring he always wore. But there is more.'

'Go on,' Jeremy prompted.

'They tried to get in touch with his people in America, through the address he had given them in the hotel register, but the address he had given turned out to be fake. That's when they got in touch with the New York police department and were duly informed that Mr. Carter was on the run from the law there. In their words, "he had a rap sheet as long as his arm for murder, extortion and blackmail."'

Rachel asked, 'But if he had given a fake address at the hotel, he could have just as easily given a fake name too. I wonder why he chose to use his own name?'

Demakis answered, 'That would not have been easy, Madame. Those were years of serious political unrest, just before the war and all foreign nationals had to register themselves at the Port Authority before entering the country. He was carrying his own passport and relevant travel documents under that name when he arrived in Greece. It was definitely Carter, who died in the fire in 1939.'

Rachel said sarcastically, 'I see. In that case, it looks as though his ghost is still carrying on the good work of murder, extortion and blackmail.'

Demakis did not get the sarcasm. 'Madame, it is too bizarre to suggest that Carter came back from the dead and wrote the notes.'

Jeremy came to his rescue, 'I think my wife was merely being facetious, Lieutenant. But you are quite right. An easier explanation would be that no self-respecting blackmailer would use his real name. Perhaps, it is someone who stayed at the Aphrodite, knew the story and used Carter's name. And I know just the fellow – Tom Preston!'

Lieutenant Demakis shook his head, 'But Mr. Preston is a highly educated, well respected and wealthy man in America. I took the liberty of getting in touch with the police in Massachusetts and I have confirmation from them that he did work in the Geology Department at Boston University and has no criminal record. Besides, I have also taken the liberty to examine his passport. He is definitely who he says he is. I still think Nikos Karalis is our man.'

Jeremy shook his head, 'It's far too pat an explanation. How we always come back to Nikos Karalis. Something tells me that we've got it the wrong way around.'

Rachel suddenly gasped, 'Jeremy! You are right. You've been telling me that we've got it the wrong way around, for some time now, and by george, we do! I see it all now, as clear as day. And it really is so simple. Oh, we've had the wool pulled over our eyes alright. The fire, the threats, the yacht. It all makes sense now, don't you see?'

'Frankly I don't, my dear.'

Rachel spoke, 'Oh, you will, darling.' Then turning to Demakis, she asked, 'Would it be possible for you and your men to gather everyone, even remotely related to this case, at the main house?'

Demakis was puzzled. 'Yes, we could but why?'

'All will be revealed when everyone is present. You must trust me on this! It simply won't work unless everyone is gathered under the same roof, and you wouldn't believe it either. It's a pity that Nikos Karalis can't be here. But your gendarme has his statements from our interrogation. And that will have to do for now. Oh my God!'

Jeremy asked, 'What? What is it?'

'I think I may have put Bilkis in terrible danger. I hope it's not too late already.'

Demakis looked perturbed. 'I don't understand what it is, you want us to do.'

Rachel spoke seriously, 'Lieutenant Demakis, please go straight to Preston's yacht and please go armed. I fear Mr. Preston will tell you that Bilkis is not on the yacht. In that case, you may need to make a thorough search of the yacht and I hope that you will find her there. There is every possibility that she is being held a prisoner, even as we speak. Whatever happens, you must find her and her little girl - Samara and bring them all back here. But time is of the essence, or you may have two more deaths on your hands. It is absolutely crucial that they be brought here. I will explain everything once you get back. Now go, please go as fast as you can.'

'Alright, alright, I will go. But I will need answers,' Demakis said.

Rachel pleaded, 'And you will get them! As soon you bring them here. For now, please make haste. Meanwhile with Jeremy's help, I shall get dressed and come up to the main house as soon as possible. We have a denouement to make.'

II

Half an hour later, the Papanos family was gathered in the sitting room of the main house. Rachel was worried and Jeremy was pacing up and down.

Suddenly the door opened and Lieutenant Demakis walked in supporting Bilkis. She looked dishevelled and had bruises on her face. Tom Preston was led in behind her. He was in handcuffs. Georgas followed, carrying Samara, who was asleep. He gently put her down on the sofa next to Rachel.

As soon as Bilkis saw Rachel, she went up to her and hugged her. 'How did you know?'

Rachel replied, 'I didn't. Not until Lieutenant Demakis returned from Athens and told me about the fire in Hotel Aphrodite. That's when everything fell in place. I am so sorry; I put you in danger without realising it.'

Bilkis responded, 'You've saved my life! He meant to kill us.'

Demakis addressed Rachel, 'I still don't understand any of this but you were right, Madame. It happened exactly as you said it would. When we reached the yacht, we found the child sleeping on the deck, possibly drugged, but Mr. Preston informed us that her mother was not on board. We went ahead and made a search anyway, as you advised, and found Miss Hamadi gagged and bound in one of the cabins below deck.'

Tom Preston spoke up gruffly, 'Look, I don't know what you two women are playing at.' Then turning to Demakis, he said, 'Can't you see? I am being framed here by these two gold digging hussies. One phone call to my uncle in America, and you will be in a lot of hot water – the lot of you, if you don't release me from this island immediately.'

Demakis walked up to Preston and looked him in the eye, 'Kidnapping is a major offence, Mr. Preston. As is assaulting a helpless woman, hence

I would suggest you keep your mouth shut for now and let Madame Rachel speak.'

Preston replied angrily, 'You damn dim-witted Greek, I'll do no such thing. I know my rights. You get me out of these handcuffs and on a telephone to America right now or I'll...'

Before he could say another word, Lieutenant Demakis' fist connected with Preston's jaw and he fell to the ground like a sack of potatoes.

Demakis spoke to the heap on the ground with authority, 'Unfortunately for you, Preston, you are in Greek custody now and you had better behave yourself or you'll find yourself in a dim-witted Greek lockup and I will personally make sure that the dim-witted key is thrown into the dim-witted Aegean Sea for all eternity. Now Madame Rachel, please explain yourself.'

Rachel spoke up, 'First of all, it was the notes that set me thinking. Yes, they definitely suggested blackmail but they also gave another picture. Life is strange and sometimes the worm turns. Let me read out the first one, which is dated two months ago. It says,

My dear Mouse, I read your last letter to me with great amusement. On the face of it, it seems, as though my meek little mouse has turned out to be a large, ungrateful and double crossing rat. As for your threats to expose me...Me of all people! I find them most amusing. Who on earth would believe you especially once I tell them about your true antecedents, along with photographic proof. I have enclosed a sample to remind you, my girl. There's plenty more where that came from. Remember the good old days? I certainly do.

It is signed Carter but most importantly, it tells us that the tables had turned on the blackmailer. The blackmailer was now being blackmailed with threats of exposure. More so, it tells us that they unnerved him to such an extent that he had to resort to sending a compromising picture to keep the "mouse" quiet for the time being.

The next note reads;

I am here. You should know well enough by now that I do not take kindly to threats. Bring the fire pearl to me at our designated meeting place today or by God, you shall answer for the consequences. 3 PM sharp. Don't keep me waiting.

Again, it is signed Carter. But this one has no date because it is clearly sent on the same day that Carter arrived on this island. He declares his presence with the opening lines – I am here. Now, the only person who arrived on this island, in the recent past, was Mr. Tom Preston. But no, if Mr. Preston was the blackmailer, he could not have sent this note on the fateful day or kept his appointment at 3PM. According to him and his girlfriend, Bilkis, they arrived much later at 9 or 10 PM. Bilkis told us that the storm had set them off course so they took shelter at the hidden cove. So they could not have been involved in Ariana's murder.

However, when we questioned Nikos Karalis about the fateful day, I will read out to you what he said. Now, this is from the notes that the gendarme took down at the lockup. When we asked Mr. Karalis if he could see the entrance to the caves at the hidden cove, his response was, "I could only see a few fishing boats and the Papanos yacht anchored there." Now, he did see a yacht on that fateful day, from his vantage point on the cliff. But it could not have been the Papanos yacht because it has come to my knowledge only recently that the Papanos yacht had been sent for repairs a month ago and was not anchored anywhere near this island. The only sensible conclusion I could draw from this, was that he had seen Mr. Preston's yacht instead on the afternoon that Ariana had disappeared. The day the storm hit the island.'

Jeremy exclaimed, 'Good lord! Is that true, Bilkis?'

Bilkis nodded, 'When we heard the news that Stanley's wife had disappeared and that there was an investigation on, Tom insisted that we tell everyone a small white lie to avoid suspicion falling on me. He said that he was only suggesting it to protect me, since I had a highly publicised history with Stanley and the Papanos family. He convinced me that the authorities might suspect that I had something to do with my ex-lover's wife's disappearance. I didn't want any trouble so I went along with it. I didn't even want to come to this island. It was Tom's idea.'

Rachel spoke, 'That is not the only white lie you told, Bilkis. Isn't it true that when I showed you the blackmail note, you immediately recognised the handwriting as Tom's?'

Bilkis responded, 'Yes, I am sorry. I didn't know what to do. Tom and I have been lovers for over a month now and I couldn't get myself to incriminate him without first asking him what it all meant, and who he wrote those notes to, using the pseudonym - Carter. That is why I made up the story of having been shocked at seeing the name of the hotel and pointed you towards Aleksy Bemus instead.'

Rachel nodded, 'I can understand that. And that was very clever of you. But when you went back last evening and questioned him, it must have given him a nasty turn. He couldn't have another woman who knew the truth. He couldn't take the chance. He had already murdered two people to hide the truth.'

Chapter Twenty One

Stavros asked, 'But why go to that extent? Killing two people just to acquire our fire pearl? Why not simply steal it?'

Rachel answered, 'It didn't have much to do with the fire pearl at all. As Jeremy intuitively kept saying, we've had it the wrong way around, from the very beginning.'

Jeremy spoke, 'Every instinct told me that all these murderous attacks had very little to do with the mere acquisition of a gem from Java. It just didn't ring true. But I still can't work out why a wealthy and educated man like Tom Preston would get involved in a sordid little game of blackmail.'

Rachel answered, 'Tom Preston is absolutely innocent. He has nothing to do with blackmail or any of this. In fact he is a victim himself, of a cruel and cunning criminal genius.'

Jeremy interjected, 'What?'

Demakis said, 'I don't understand.'

Rachel motioned towards Tom Preston and said, 'Ladies and gentlemen, might I introduce Mr. Andrew Carter to you all. A desperate murderer, extortionist and blackmailer, who has been running from the long arm of the law for the past few decades. He has a vast criminal record. He did meet an American geologist called Tom Preston, perhaps at the bar of the Aphrodite Hotel and then I can only surmise what happened. After they had both had a few drinks, Tom Preston must have told him his life's story – how he was an only child, or that he missed not having a family since both his parents were dead, and a little story about his estranged uncle back in America – the millionaire Richie Preston, a man he had never met. Carter immediately saw an opportunity. Tom Preston's parents were dead. He had no other kith and kin. No one would miss him.

I presume he must have drugged the man, stolen his passport, travel documents, luggage and papers. Then put Preston in Carter's bed, put his signet ring on Tom's finger and set fire to Carter's hotel room. Carter woke in Tom Preston's room the next day and took on his identity. I assume they were about the same height with similar features, otherwise he could not have gotten away with. The end result being that he had provided himself with a new identity and fresh start at life. He must have left Greece shortly after that for America before anyone at the hotel realised the truth. The millionaire uncle – Richie Preston, taking a shine to him was just an additional gamble that paid off.'

Stanley asked, 'How does Ariana fit into all of this?'

'Carter was a disreputable character and a regular patron at the hotel, where Ariana worked as a waitress. And I can only surmise that he probably took a fancy to her and then using some foul method, perhaps by inviting her out and drugging her food or drink, he took her to his room. He took compromising pictures of her and then he used them to blackmail and manipulate the poor girl for the rest of her life.'

Stanley spoke, 'No wonder she was so secretive about her life before she met me.'

Rachel continued, 'I think that after the fire at Hotel Aphrodite when Carter left for America, she must have been truly relieved to be out of his vile clutches. She started stepping out with a young man called Nikos. But then Carter came back to Greece as Tom Preston, she had no choice but to go to him whenever he made demands on her. Which is why Nikos thought that she was cheating on him with an older man. She wasn't. She was just being blackmailed into being with a man she despised. But soon she realised that she held an equal power over him.'

Lieutenant Demakis said slowly as the truth became clear to him, 'He killed her because she could expose his true identity to the uncle - Richie Preston.'

'Exactly! You see, she knew that he was Andrew Carter and she knew that he was using a false identity. When she came to know that he was hoping to come into an inheritance worth millions using his false identity, she probably began to threaten him with her knowledge. Perhaps she thought that she could blackmail him, in turn, to return her compromising photographs, which he held in possession. But with her threats to expose him, she signed her own death warrant. I suspect she intuitively knew the danger she was in, hence her note to Karalis, to be by her side when she handed over the fire pearl to Carter and took back the damning photographs. That was probably the deal she had made with Carter.

But it all went horribly wrong for her when she got caught by Aristea or someone else in the family as she was stealing the fire pearl. And then Karalis didn't show up. I believe she still went ahead and met Carter. Perhaps to foolishly plead for more time to get him the fire pearl but she never realised that his true motive all along had been to meet her in an isolated spot and kill her. He used the fire pearl as bait to avoid revealing his true intentions. After all, an inheritance worth millions was at stake. If Richie Preston got wind of the fact that his nephew was an imposter, Carter could kiss his prospective millionaire status goodbye. You know the rest.'

Tom Preston started laughing, 'You've got quite an imagination, woman, I'll give you that. But you forget that you have no proof at all, for any of this.'

Rachel smirked, 'That will not be too difficult, I assure you. All we need are some file pictures of Andrew Carter from the New York police department. Plus, I am sure, Nikos Karalis will be able to pull you out of a line-up when he's reminded about the older man he saw with his girlfriend at Athens.'

'Bullshit! I've been here a week and met him and I can tell you, that man didn't recognise me.'

'Perhaps you wore your hat with its brim hanging low, whenever you came face to face with him in the past week. Or it could be that you've changed your hair colour, taken off a beard or a moustache. I don't know. We'll have to ask Karalis about it. But there are many other ways to make an identification, you know. Tom Preston actually studied at Boston University and he had classmates, and later colleagues in his Geology department, who will be able to recognise that fact that you are not Tom Preston. I believe Boston University has a pretty strong alma mater. If that doesn't work, they could show your photograph to his neighbours and people he knew in Boston. The possibilities are endless. But we'll just let the authorities decide what to do with you, shall we?' Rachel said, as she smiled sweetly at him.

Carter was livid, 'You lousy, snooping hussy. I should have hit you harder and finished you off when I had the chance.'

Rachel smiled, 'Thank you for your confession. You did attack to kill me but you didn't reckon that I'd survive the blow. And now I know why you attacked me. It was because I had casually let it drop when we visited you on the yacht that I knew someone at Boston University. And that I would write to them about meeting you in Greece. Even a simple thing like that made you panic. You are such a pathetic and insecure person, living a life of lies that I almost feel sorry for you.'

'Go to hell!'

Rachel continued, 'You were never on the cliff that day. Marina almost caught sight of you on the property, didn't she, as she was coming out of the water. You managed to hide from her just in time and then tried to pin my attack on her. You are good at this sort of thing. As they say practice makes perfect. You tried to frame Nikos by stealing his shirt. I bet you stole it from the clothesline outside his house, as it was drying. You wore it to kill Ariana and then planted the bloodstained shirt in his store.'

Carter growled, 'You can't pin anything on me.'

'Oh yes, I can. You've already admitted to attacking me. Just like you attacked the maid Dorkas when she saw you steal the fire pearl and tried to blackmail you?'

Bilkis spoke up, 'No, that was me. I stole the fire pearl but I didn't kill Dorkas, I swear. You see, I crashed a vase by accident, as I was leaving through the window.'

Marina spoke, 'That was you? We all thought it was Moussaka!'

Demakis asked, 'Now, who is Moussaka?'

Marina deadpanned, 'Our cat, Lieutenant. I hope you are not going to arrest her.'

Bilkis ignored her and continued, 'Dorkas saw me as I left through the window and tried to blackmail me later that night. She came to the yacht to ask for money. I gave her some cash to keep her quiet and she went away. But I told Tom what had happened and that I feared she may go to the police even after having taken the money. He told me not to worry and that he'd take care of it. He must have followed her and...'

Rachel asked, 'But later, the next morning when you heard she had been killed, you still didn't put two and two together?'

Bilkis spoke, 'Of course, I asked him about it. Right after you and Jeremy left the yacht and he denied it outright. He told me that it must have been the work of the murderous lunatic running loose on the island. You must think me very stupid but I believed him and that is the truth.'

Stavros asked Bilkis, 'Why did you steal the fire pearl?'

She answered matter-of-factly, 'To take revenge on your family. Stanley refused to acknowledge that he was the father of my child even after I came pleading to him six years ago, when I found out I was pregnant. I was hoping we could marry and raise a family together. And what did he do? He sent his grandmother to deal with me. She treated me like a prostitute and offered me money to leave him alone. I know how much you all prize that fire pearl. Stanley had told me about it, in our happier days together.'

Aristea asked, 'So you waited all these years to steal the fire pearl? I don't understand it. Why?'

Bilkis said, 'Ask your precious grandson.'

When Stanley stayed mute, Bilkis continued, 'Too ashamed to talk, I see. After I paid you all a visit the other day, he visited me on the boat later that night and told me to get off his island. He told me didn't want anything to do with me or my "bastard child" as he put it.'

Aristea spoke with anger, 'Is this true, Stanley?'

Stanley looked at the floor but didn't say a word.

Rachel spoke softly, stroking Samara's hair, as she slept by her side, 'I know it's not my place, Aristea, but may I add that Samara is a beautiful child and quite the spitting image of her father.'

Aristea said, 'I am sorry, Bilkis. I had no idea. If only I had known that the child was really his...'

Bilkis gave a hollow laugh, 'Oh, you don't have to grovel, Madame. Don't worry. I'll give you your precious fire pearl back. I did it for a lark anyway. And I don't want to have anything further to do with your spineless grandson either.'

Jeremy asked, 'But if this is the truth then why were you all so scared to tell me what happened the day Ariana disappeared?'

Aristea spoke, 'Marina caught her stealing the fire pearl. I retrieved it from her and informed Stanley. He was so furious that he hit her. I overheard him tell Ariana that he had had enough of her lies. He told her to pack her things and get out of the house and off this island within the hour or he would kill her. She was frightened. There was a storm coming and we practically threw her out.'

Marina spoke, 'I'm not proud of it now but I stood at her door, watching as Ariana hastily put some things together in a bedspread. She asked me where she could go and I told her I didn't care, as long as she left the house. I advised her not to go into the village and create a scene because that would only infuriate Stanley more, but to take a boat from our boathouse and head for Patra.'

Aristea added, 'None of us realised it would be such a terrible storm. Later, when the storm was at its peak, I sent Marina out into the gale to check if

Ariana was still there in the boat house. I asked her to bring her back if she was still there. But while there was no sign of Ariana, Marina noticed that one of the speedboats was missing. She also found Ariana's belongings tied in the bedspread inside the boathouse. Fearing the worst, she brought the bundle back to the house and I instructed her to hide it in our shed the next day until we could dispose it off.'

Demakis asked, 'What about the blood spatters in the boat house?'

Marina spoke sheepishly, 'That was me. My dress got caught on a nail and when I tried to remove it, a shard of rotted wood snapped out and slashed my forearm. I bleed easily. There was blood everywhere.'

Stavros said, 'You told me Moussaka had scratched you.'

Marina shrugged and Rachel spoke, 'So that's how Ariana's things ended up in the shed. And more importantly, it also explains why she ended up in the sea. She must have taken the boat to the other side of the island before the storm to meet Carter. He slit her throat, put her in the boat and pushed it out on to the sea, where it must have capsized, once the storm blew in. I suppose she had planned to return to the boathouse after her meeting with Carter and then take her belongings up to Nikos' place. Perhaps the poor girl thought that she could beg him to give her shelter for the night.'

Marina spoke, 'Well, it's a great relief to us anyhow, to know that at any rate, we didn't send her to her death. All this while, we thought we did.'

Stavros shook his head, 'Heartless. Poor Ariana may have married my brother but she was never truly made to feel like one of the family. I love my family but they really are heartless. All of them. Absolutely heartless!'

Epilogue

*T*he next day, Lieutenant Demakis left the island with his prisoner - Tom Preston a.k.a. Andrew Carter in handcuffs. His idea was to bring him face to face with Nikos Karalis for a positive identification but that was rendered unnecessary as Carter confessed to his crimes.

Jeremy later informed Rachel that after a night in the lockup under Lieutenant Demakis' kind ministrations, which left Carter with a broken nose and two missing teeth, the prisoner had lost his bluster and kindly consented to give them a written statement of confession for all his crimes in Greece. When Jeremy asked Demakis if he would get into trouble for roughing up the suspect in custody, Demakis had responded with a straight face,

'What are you talking about? We don't believe in coercion. That man must have fallen down some stairs.'

Stavros and Marina had very kindly offered Rachel and Jeremy a cruise to Patra on their yacht. When Bilkis returned the fire pearl to Aristea, the grand old lady insisted that both Bilkis and Samara join them on the cruise. Bilkis had graciously accepted. They had to pack and leave the island anyway since Tom Preston's yacht was going to be moved away by the Hellenic Gendarmerie later that day.

Stanley had refused to come along with them on the cruise and stayed back at the house brooding at the waves from his window. Recent events had evidently left him with a lot to think about. He hadn't even bothered to come out and say goodbye to them.

Later, on the cruise, Rachel noticed that Aristea and Samara got along like a house on fire. Jeremy noticed it too. He whispered to Rachel, 'If that old lady doesn't leave everything she owns to that great grandchild of hers, I'll eat my hat.' Just thinking about it made Rachel smile. She had grown very fond of Samara herself.

Once they reached Patra, Jeremy and Rachel informed the family that they wished to say their final goodbyes and disembark at Patra. They had impulsively decided to meet Dr. Christos once more before heading out to see the temple at Delphi. They planned to play it by ear from there with some light travel and a spot of sightseeing before they could catch the boat home in a week's time.

All-in-all, Greece had been a bittersweet experience for them in so many ways and Rachel sighed once they were finally on the boat back to England.

Yes, it had been quite an experience but now all she really wanted, was to sit in her favourite armchair beside Jeremy, in front of a crackling log fire with Toby on her lap, as the rain clattered down.

~ THE END ~

CPSIA information can be obtained
at www.ICGtesting.com
Printed in the USA
LVHW091548251021
701482LV00009B/367